Touch
Me Now

Touch Me Now

DONNA HILL

HARLEQUIN®

entertain, enrich, inspire™

Recycling programs
for this product may
not exist in your area.

TOUCH ME NOW

ISBN-13: 978-0-373-53483-8

Copyright © 2012 by Donna Hill

www.Harlequin.com

Printed in U.S.A.

Dear Reader,

Welcome to the lush and often lavish world of Sag Harbor, New York, steeped in rich African American history, folklore and romance. I felt this was the perfect place to set my latest series, Sag Harbor Village, and introduce you to new faces as well as reacquaint you with some familiar ones.

As many of you may recall in *Dare to Dream,* Desiree Armstrong and Lincoln Davenport found each other in Sag Harbor. Melanie Harte from *Heart's Reward,* owner of The Platinum Society, has a mansion on the hills of Sag Harbor. And of course there is Rafe Lawson from my Lawsons of Louisiana series, who frequents the services of Melanie's matchmaking enterprise.

Now I would love to introduce you to my latest visitors to Sag Harbor: the talented masseuse Layla Brooks, godsister to Melanie and soror to Desiree, and the über sexy and mysterious navy SEAL Maurice Lawson. Yes, you have the name right. Maurice is the nephew of Senator Branford Lawson!

So sit back, put up your feet and let me take you on a journey of sensual pleasure, life-changing discoveries and the healing of the heart and soul in my latest offering, *Touch Me Now.*

Happy reading,

Donna

Prologue

It was late afternoon. The lunch crowd, what there had been of it, was gone. Business was slow, slower than usual for this time of year. Everyone was hurting, it seemed. She'd been let go from the paper months earlier, but had been lucky enough to pick up a few extra hours at Jack and Jill's the local lounge and jazz spot in the West Village, and she had begun to build a pretty solid list of clients from her massage business thanks to Brent.

Thoughts of Brent brought a smile to her face and a rush of sensual excitement through her veins. There were times when she still wondered how she'd gotten so lucky. Brent had women running after him like a buy-two-get-one-free sale at Macy's. But she was the one that he wanted. He'd proved it to her time and again and there wasn't a day that went by that he didn't tell her that he loved her or did something to show her.

She wiped down the tables and glanced with a sense of awe at the dazzling diamond on the third finger of her left hand. In six months she would join the ranks of her girls Melanie and Desiree and become a married woman. She'd picked out her dress. Simple and elegant Desiree had said. It was going to be a small, intimate wedding, only their really close friends and immediate family. Melanie offered her place at Sag Harbor for the wedding and reception. Layla couldn't wait to be Mrs. Brent Davis.

"Daydreaming again?" Mona asked, sidling up next to her. Mona Clarke ran Jack and Jill's and in the six months that Layla worked there, they'd become more than employer/employee, they'd become friends. Mona completely understood that Layla's job at the lounge was only temporary and that her real love was the art of massage, the power to heal through touch.

Layla turned and a shy smile teased her full lip-glossed mouth. "That bad?"

"Yes, very," Mona said, with her fist on her hip. "Hey, I got this." She took the cloth from Layla's hand. "It's slow as maple syrup in here today. Why don't you go on home to your man, see what he can do about that cheery disposition of yours," she teased.

"You sure?"

"Yeah, go ahead. Unless you really need the tips you're not going to make today. Go, go, practice some of your massage techniques on that fine specimen."

Layla wiggled her brows. "Hmm, maybe I will." She gave Mona a quick kiss on the cheek. "I owe you," she called out as she hurried to the back to get her purse.

"See you on the weekend."

Layla stopped at the local market on her way home and picked up some fresh vegetables and seasonings for a stir fry meal and a bottle of Brent's favorite wine. She still had a few hours to prepare everything before Brent got off work. She wanted things to be extra special. In fact she planned to take Mona up on her suggestion and try out a new massage technique on him that she'd been mastering and maybe that new Victoria's Secret lingerie that she'd splurged on. A wicked thought tickled her belly.

With her purchases in hand she strolled the four blocks to her apartment, intermittently stopping to check out the window displays at boutiques and artisanal shops along the way.

She climbed the stairs to her walk-up and came to a dead stop at the front door, momentarily alarmed by the sound of movement inside until she heard

Brent's voice. She let go of a breath of relief. Calling 911 would have really screwed up her afternoon. Brent home early. The surprise was on her.

Layla turned her key in the door all ready to leap into Brent's arms but came to a grinding halt when she saw Brent and two suitcases in the middle of the floor.

He slowly turned to her with his cell phone still at his ear. There was a look in his hazel eyes that defied explanation. She'd never seen it before or since—her own terror, disbelief and pain reflected in someone else's eyes.

All he said was that he was sorry. He couldn't do this. He didn't love her. He never wanted to hurt her. He was leaving.

She was certain she'd screamed, threw things, demanded answers, maybe she even begged him not to leave. Who knows? None of it changed anything, anyway. He was gone.

What was she going to do now with the pieces of her heart scattered all over her hardwood floors and her soul on the other side of the door walking into a life without her?

Chapter 1

One Year Later...

Summer came early to New York. Memorial Day was three weeks away and the temperature was already in the low eighties. If this was any indication of what the next three months would bring it was going to be a long, hot summer in the city.

Layla Brooks sat on the sill of her third floor walk-up apartment of the prewar building that faced Washington Square Park. She peered out of the smudged window at the entanglement of humanity on the streets below. Absently she fanned herself with the stiff, white envelope that boasted a Sag Harbor address—a world away from where she lived in the West Village.

The West Village was known for its eclectic blend of people, styles, food, excitement and entertainment. Those were the things that drew her to this slice of New York City life, that and her cushy job as a journalist for *The View*. Her beat was New York lifestyles and in search of the next salacious story she haunted some of the best and the worst locales in the city.

It was simply ironic how things got twisted all around and she became her own headline: laid off, unemployment running out, and working two nights a week as a hostess at Jake and Jill's one of the local blues lounges. All things considered, she was better off than a lot of folks. She'd saved her money over the years and invested wisely, thanks to the wise counsel of her godmother Carolyn Harte. The paper had given her a decent severance and in the year that she'd been out of work, she'd finally finished up her classes in massage therapy. It had been an on-again, off-again process for nearly five years. Now she was fully certified in rehabilitation therapy, deep tissue massage and she had even taken a special course, two years earlier in tantric massage, which was how she'd met Brent Davis, her former fiancé.

Brent was the manager of the tantric massage studio, tucked away in a three-story townhouse on the Lower East Side. He'd trained her—*personally*. There was no question that in the right hands the eroticism of the human touch is mind-blowing. Unfortunately, Brent felt the same way—about *every-*

one. She'd been naïve and in love, engaged to be married to the man of her dreams and too blind to see that Brent didn't only have "hands" for her. It took her a while to push that part of her life to the back of her head. But the hurt would rear its ugly head every now and again when she'd see couples hugged up together, whispering to each other and knowing that the evening would end with them in bed together—and she would roll around alone on empty sheets.

The upside was that Brent was good at what he did and he'd taught her everything she needed to know to be just as good a masseuse as him, if not better. She had a few regular clients and the extra income was great. The idea of owning and running a studio became more intriguing day by day. But with the economy still on shaky ground she wasn't quite ready to take the leap. At least not yet.

She stopped fanning herself and flipped the envelope over. She ran her finger beneath the flap and tore it open. She pulled out the stiff, off-white postcard inside.

It was the invitation she'd been expecting, embossed with the Platinum Society logo. It was the kickoff party of the season coupled with Desiree and Lincoln's fifth wedding anniversary party, hosted by Layla's god-sister, Melanie Harte. Although the festivities were more than a month away, Mel always planned way in advance.

Desiree Armstrong was her soror and dear friend. They still laughed about all the fun they used to have as students living in the Big Apple. So when Desiree married Lincoln Davenport and moved out to Sag Harbor to open her art gallery and help out with his Bed & Breakfast establishment, The Port, Layla and Desiree didn't see each other as often as they once did, but Layla could always find a reason to visit Sag Harbor.

She'd spent most of her summers on the Harbor. Her godmother, Carolyn, the cofounder of the Platinum Society—a high class matchmaking service— made sure that she kept an eye on her precocious daughter Melanie, and Melanie didn't go far without Layla. They'd grown up rubbing elbows with the people that the average person only saw on television and in the news. Melanie and Layla were trained in the areas of entertainment, money management, travel, fashion and knowing how to mix and mingle with anyone from the man on the street to the President of the United States. Like Melanie, Layla could speak three languages fluently and had traveled to Europe and Africa before she was eighteen. And if Layla had her way she would have married Melanie's gorgeous brother Alan even though he always thought of her as the "cute kid," and his little sister's friend.

She smiled as those good memories rushed to the surface before she hopped down from the sill, just as a truck backfired below and let off a plume of smoke into the muggy air.

Yes, it would be great to get away. A change of scenery, hanging with her girls and enjoying a blow-out party was just what she needed.

"I think you should stay for the summer," Desiree was saying while she held the cell phone between her jaw and shoulder and adjusted a painting on the wall.

"Girl, the whole summer! You have got to be kidding. I have…stuff up here to take care of."

"Yeah, right. What *stuff*—a hostess job?"

"I have clients. They'll miss me," she said, trying to sound convincing.

"I have a beach full of clients for you and you know Melanie will hook you up. Besides, when was the last time that the three of us had a chance to spend some real time together?"

Layla thought about the tempting offer. But the truth was, both of her girls were married; Desiree to Lincoln and Melanie to Claude. She would be the proverbial fifth wheel. Her chest tightened as images of what could have been flashed for an instant in front of her.

"I don't know, Desi," she said slowly, teetering on the brink of relenting.

Desiree blew out a puff of frustration. "Well, whatever you decide to do is fine. I think you're blowing a perfectly good vacation."

"Where would I stay for the entire summer?"

"Right here at The Port."

"Desi, come on. What about your guests? The summer is the busiest season. You need all of your guesthouses."

"True, but you wouldn't be a guest."

"What are you talking about?"

"You would be a summer employee."

"I thought you said this was my vacation." She chuckled.

"Look, what if you stayed in one of the cottages and paid your way by offering massages to my guests? I've had a spa set up for months with no one to really run it. It would be a major perk. And you get to keep the tips!"

Layla burst out laughing. Desiree always had some kind of plan. "Let me think about it."

"Okay, but don't think too long. I know someone will want to hop on this great opportunity."

"Someone like whom?"

"Doesn't matter. Someone will."

"Girl, you are too crazy."

"Crazy as a fox," Desiree said with a snicker.

"Yeah, okay. Anyhow, I'll see you next weekend. But I'll let you know before then what I'm going to do."

"See you next week. And think about the offer. It's perfect."

"Okay, okay. I'll think about it. I'll see you Friday."

"Smooches."

Layla disconnected the call. *An entire summer on the Harbor*? Hmmm. She got up from the side of the bed and walked toward the window. She pushed the off white curtain aside. Traffic, gray concrete and throngs of rushing people filled her line of sight.

She let the curtain drop back in place. A slow smile lifted the corners of her mouth. Nothing was keeping her in the city beyond her decision to just say yes.

Chapter 2

Maurice Lawson winced when he attempted to push up from the couch and stand. The pain in his leg vibrated through his entire body. He squeezed his eyes shut and gritted his teeth. Slowly the searing fire ebbed to a dull throb. He inhaled deeply and sat back down.

That night, flying over the Afghanistan mountains flashed in his head. The skies were clear with just enough cloud cover to camouflage their mission. He and his Navy SEAL crew were on a stealth mission. Everything was going according to plan. The target was illuminated on the control panel of the Black Hawk Helicopter. And then without warning the world seemed to explode. He'd lost two men on that mission and he'd barely survived himself. He'd spent three months in the hospital and the next three months in rehab, learning how to walk again.

The doctors said he'd always have pain…and nightmares. But over time both would diminish. They hadn't.

That was more than a year ago. He still battled the pain and the nightmares…and the guilt. Some days, the guilt was more painful than his injury.

"Maurice…"

He opened his eyes and his gaze settled on Dr. Morrison.

"Are you all right?" She put down her pad.

He nodded. "Yeah." He forced a laugh. "I should be used to it by now."

"How are you sleeping?"

He shrugged. "Some nights are better than others I suppose."

Maurice Lawson had been referred to her through the Veterans Administration. After recovering from his wounds it was clear that his injuries were more than physical. She'd been working with him for about six months and the psychotherapy was slow, but there were days when she felt they were making progress. Then there were days like this one when that haunted look would come into his eyes.

Dr. Morrison leaned forward. "Maurice, your physical therapy is over, but I can't get you beyond that night if you won't let me help you to help yourself. You're holding on to more than physical pain and that's what's really debilitating."

The corners of his eyes pinched. His full mouth drew into a tight line. "What do you want from me?"

"I want you to accept that what happened that night was not your fault."

"But it was!" he bellowed. "Why can't you understand that? I was in charge. Those men relied on me to get them in and out of there safely. And I didn't."

"What could you have done differently?" she softly asked.

He turned away from her penetrating stare. He'd asked himself that very question a million times. He'd gone over every minute of that flight. Nothing stuck out. It was textbook. But he had to have missed something. And that's what haunted him.

"What?" she asked again.

"I don't know," he finally answered, his voice filled with defeat. "I don't know."

"How about your friends, family, have you been in touch with them?"

"We don't have anything in common. They all want to act as if nothing is wrong or that everything is." His laugh was ragged.

"You can't continue to live in your head, Maurice, disconnected from everything. It's well past the time that you rejoined the world. Begin new relationships."

"Is that right, Doc," he said derisively. "You mean

if I join the world, as you put it, I'll be *all* better." This time he fought against the pain and stood.

"I'm saying that you can't continue to punish yourself by shutting everything and everyone out."

"It's not that easy," he said, gritting his teeth against the pain.

"I know it's not. It never is. But if you are ever going to regain some semblance of life, of an existence, you're going to have to try. You're going to have to work at it, just as hard and with just as much passion as you've put into being a decorated fighter pilot."

He stole a look at her. "I don't know how," he admitted.

Dr. Morrison stood up and came to him. "I have a friend who owns a fabulous Bed & Breakfast in Sag Harbor. I think a change of scenery and the relaxation of being by the water would be therapeutic."

"I don't think so, Doc."

"At least think about it, Maurice. And I'll only be a phone call away...when you want to talk."

He pushed out a breath. "Yeah, I'll think about it."

She returned to her desk and wrote the information down on a prescription pad, tore off the paper and handed it to him.

He looked at the neat handwriting. "The Port."

"Go, Maurice. A few days, a few weeks." She studied his face. "Give yourself a chance. And think about getting back in touch with Ross."

His gaze jumped to hers.

"You'd mentioned in earlier sessions that the two of you were close, that you even played in a band together. I'm sure he would be glad to hear from you. Have you spoken to him since you've been home?"

He lowered his head. "No." He folded the paper and shoved it in his pants pocket. "Time up?"

She moistened her lips. "Yes."

He bobbed his head. His jaw clenched as he turned toward the door. "See you next week, Doc."

Maurice opened the door to his one bedroom condo apartment. He'd lucked out and was able to purchase the condo from his Veterans benefits in one of the most sought after communities in the quickly gentrifying neighborhood of Ft. Greene. One of the perks of fighting for your country, he thought derisively.

He'd been in the space for nearly a year after leaving rehab and it was still sparsely furnished, only the basic necessities. It didn't matter much to him. It was only him. He didn't have company, there was no woman in his life and all he needed was a place to sleep, eat and bathe.

He tossed his keys into a plastic bowl on the kitchen counter and limped over to the window. He drew in a long, slow breath. Never in a million years would he have imagined his life coming to this point. His breathing echoed in the cavernous space. *Alone. Broken.*

Dr. Morrison's words bounced around in his head. *…if you are ever going to regain some semblance of life, of an existence, you're going to have to try. You're going to have to work at it, just as hard and with just as much passion as you've put into being a decorated fighter pilot….And think about getting back in touch with Ross.*

Ross. He almost smiled. Ross McDaniels was his best buddy all through high school and into college. They discovered their love of music together and that it was a surefire way to charm the ladies. Ross was the sax man, he the piano. The two of them together were a lethal combination. Ross had been in his corner when he lost his father and never once came down on him for cutting himself off from his family, even if he didn't agree. They'd stayed in touch throughout his years in the service and it was not until the accident that Maurice cut off all contact. He didn't think he could stand to see the look of sympathy in Ross's eyes. That, he knew he could not take.

He slung his hands into his pockets. Ross didn't deserve that. His stomach muscles clenched. Was his number still the same? He pulled his cell phone from his pocket and scrolled through his contact list.

Ross McDaniels. What could he possibly say to him after all this time?

Maurice swallowed over the tight knot in his throat. Ross had a birthday coming up. His was a month earlier to the day and Ross used to always tease him about being "the oldest."

He stared at the number, debated a million reasons why and why not and finally pressed Call before he could change his mind.

The line rang three times before it was picked up. "Hello?"

"Hey, Ross, it's me…Maurice."

For a moment the line went completely silent.

"Mo…" he finally said. "Don't B.S. me, man, is this really you?"

The tight knot in his gut burst loose and a tentative smile tugged at his lips. "Yeah, man, it's me. You usually have impersonators calling you?"

Ross laughed from deep down in his belly, a sound so welcome and familiar. Maurice's eyes stung.

"Not usually. I…where the hell are you?"

"In Brooklyn."

"Brooklyn? You're back? Why haven't you called? I tried to find you for months. The Navy wouldn't tell me shit. What happened? How long have you been home, man?"

Maurice waited a beat. "I've been home a little over a year," he said quietly.

He could almost see the waves of confusion pass over Ross's face as he tried to process what he'd just been told.

"Say what?"

"It's a long story. I…would have…I should have called…"

"I'm gonna forget that I should be pissed as hell right now. Brother, I thought…we all thought you were dead, man."

Maurice heard Ross's voice crack and that nearly broke him. "Look, I had my reasons."

"I'm listening. No, as a matter of fact, this is not for a phone conversation. I want to put my eyes on you. Where are you in Brooklyn?"

"Fort Greene. Why?"

"You driving?"

"Yeah."

"Janet is throwing me a little birthday party tonight. I want you here."

"Ross…man…"

"I'll text you the address. Eight o'clock. Not taking no for an answer. Besides, I spent enough birthdays without my man at my side."

He thought about it. "Things are different. I'm different."

"We all are," he said softly. "Eight o'clock."

"All right. Eight."

Chapter 3

Layla was never one for sitting in traffic and knew that city dwellers would be packing up to head to the shores come Friday afternoon. The idea of bumper to bumper cars, noise and horn blowing put her spine in a vice grip. She decided to hit the road on Thursday at mid-day. Getting around the winding streets of lower Manhattan was half the battle. Once she hit the William Floyd Parkway toward Shirley, Long Island it got easier. She put her foot down on the gas and didn't let up.

The two and a half-hour drive took just about two hours and before she had a chance to get tired she saw the signs for the Sag Harbor turnoff up ahead.

She pressed the button on the armrest to lower the

windows and took a deep inhale of the ocean-tinged air. The scents of salt, sand and sea were carried along by the balmy breeze. Layla inhaled deeply. Her grip loosened on the steering wheel and her shoulders slowly lowered from their sentinel position near her neck. She had no idea how tightly wound her body was until she felt the embrace of the leather cushion of the seat.

Her clients were lukewarm about her departure and one woman began to whine about how Layla's leaving was interfering with her calendar. Mona told her that her job at Jack and Jill's would be waiting for her when she got back and not to worry about a thing. Mona had lent strong shoulder strength after the utter devastation of her engagement to Brent. Mona spent many an hour and drank countless mimosas listening to Layla pour out her heartache and fury and just as many assuring her that it was Brent who was the asshole, that it was his loss not hers and that a real man was out there waiting for her—when she was ready. She was certain she would never be ready. She couldn't survive another hurt like that and the only way to get hurt like that is to love someone. That was something she had no more intentions of doing. She was going to build her business, travel, enjoy her friends and maybe even write a book one day about the art of healing through touch. But love…she was done.

She'd paid up her rent for three months, had her

utilities and cable temporarily suspended, packed her bags and hit the road. Taking in the magnificent view and allowing the tranquility of the shore to seep into her limbs, she knew she'd made the right decision.

Her foot eased off the accelerator as she entered the town proper. The cobblestone streets were lined with bright colored canopies and shiny glass windows advertising the array of shops, restaurants, bakeries, specialty stores and art galleries. The waters along the pier were home to everything from basic fishing boats, to outboards to large yachts and party boats that lolled atop the soft waves.

The Port was beyond the center of town, across a wide swath of beach and soft rolling hills. Lincoln had built the place up from two small cabins to a dozen, complete with the kind of amenities expected at high price hotels—a bar, sit down restaurant, exercise room, a lounge and room service. And now The Port had its own masseuse.

Layla followed the winding streets out of the main part of town until the shops began to recede in her rearview mirror. The summer homes, and for some, yearlong homes, began to dot the landscape with pops of color against the sandy shores and green slopes.

Twenty minutes later she was driving onto The Port property. She pulled into an available parking space and got out. She arched her back and stretched her arms high over her head then took a look around.

Not much had changed that she could determine since the last time she'd visited. But knowing Desiree and Lincoln, *Mr. & Mrs. DIY*, she was sure that there were many new changes yet to be discovered.

Layla grabbed her oversized purse from the passenger seat, shut the car door and walked into the reception area.

A gorgeous young woman who looked as if she'd been carved out of polished ebony wood greeted her.

"Welcome to The Port. My name is Gina. Do you have a reservation or would you like a tour?"

"Hello, Gina. Umm, I'm actually a friend of Desi and Lincoln. I'm going to be doing massage therapy for the summer."

Gina's brows lifted and her lush mouth widened into a brilliant smile displaying two rows of even white teeth. "Of course. Mrs. Davenport told me to expect you. Let me tell her you're here." She picked up a phone on the desk, spoke briefly then glanced up at Layla. "Follow me, Ms. Brooks."

Much of what Layla remembered since her last visit was the same. The Port was still a classy place, from the high-end furnishings to the sense of elegance, style and professionalism that seemed to ooze from the staff. She did notice some new artwork, and a humungous flat screen television that served as an entertainment medium, and also provided updates about The Port and the town of Sag Harbor that scrolled across the bottom.

Layla followed Gina down the short hallway to where she remembered Desiree's office to be. Gina tapped lightly on the partially opened door.

"Come in," rang out the cheery voice.

"Your friend Ms. Brooks is here." Gina headed back to the front.

Before Layla could put one foot in front of the other the door swung fully open and Desiree burst out like sunshine after a storm.

"Layla!" Desiree swept her friend up in a tight hug then stepped back and held her at arm's length. "How was the drive?"

"A breeze. You look fabulous. And happy."

Desiree had opted for a short, natural spiral hairstyle and her complexion fairly glowed from the inside out.

"Thanks and I am." She beamed, then a frown tightened her brow. She glanced around the space where Layla stood. "Where are your bags?"

"In the car."

"Oh," she breathed in relief, pressing her hand to her chest. "For a minute I thought you weren't planning to stay." She hooked her arm through Layla's. "Let's get your bags and I'll show you where you'll be staying."

"I'm not sure for how long, but I have enough clothes and accessories to last me a minute."

Desiree laughed. "Now that's what I'm talking about."

They walked arm-in-arm out of the main building and across the landscaped front. Desiree had one of the staff gather Layla's bags from her car and bring them to her room.

"I'm so glad that you decided to come," Desiree said while she turned the key in the cottage door lock. "You're going to love it and my guests are going to love you." She swung the door open and they stepped inside.

As Layla expected, the space was beautiful. Pale walls and whitewashed floors gave the rooms an expansive, open aired feeling and the rattan furnishings, glass accessories and the bay windows topped it off. Although The Port had a full-service restaurant and bar as well as room service, each cabin came with its own fully functional kitchen.

Layla's cabin looked out onto the beach and down the pathway that branched right and left with a cabin on each side of comparable size to hers.

She dropped her purse on the kitchen counter and turned toward Desiree with a broad smile on her face. "Beautiful."

Desiree took a mock bow. "And you're going to have a ball. I'll leave you to get settled. When you're ready come on over to the main building. Lincoln can't wait to see you."

"Okay. Give me about an hour."

"See you then."

Desiree let herself out and Layla took her bags to

the bedroom and began to unpack. She laid out an outfit and then went into the bathroom for a quick shower.

Wrapped in a thick, pale peach towel, Layla padded around her new digs and she had to admit, from the moment that she'd stepped onto the property and inhaled the ocean-washed air and spectacular views, she felt lighter inside. All of the worry and stress of everything related to home evaporated. She went into the seating area and turned on the stereo, and then two-stepped to the beat back into her bedroom.

Totally refreshed, and dressed for the sultry spring afternoon, Layla followed the path back to the main building and took in the sights along the way.

Maurice Lawson lounged beneath the shade of the blue and white striped canopy that hung above his back deck. His injured leg was elevated on a pillow. Absently, he rubbed his upper thigh while he watched the waves gently move in and out from the shore. The temperature was perfect, and the light breeze blowing off the water combined for a near hypnotic effect. Although he'd been reluctant to take his therapist's advice, he was glad that he'd come. The past few nights were the first in months that he wasn't awakened by the nightmares. Simply being able to rest through the night was beginning to have a positive effect on his spirit.

It was hooking up with Ross that finally changed his mind.

There'd been several moments of panic when he'd pulled up in front of Ross's Long Island home. He'd sat in his car debating on whether to get out and go inside. But then the front door to the house opened and Ross stepped out and all the time apart slipped away. It didn't matter to Ross and Janet that he'd been hurt or that he'd cut them off for so long or that he was seeing a shrink to try to get his head right. All that mattered was that their friend was alive and he was back.

He and Ross talked long after the last guest went home. They talked until the sun rose, and when he returned to his apartment in Brooklyn he felt almost human. Human enough to take Ross and Janet and Dr. Morrison's advice and go to Sag Harbor. Do some thinking and some soul searching. And whatever he decided, they would be there for him when he returned.

He rested his head against the back of the chair and was just about to close his eyes and let the pain medication settle in when movement to his right drew his attention. At first he thought that perhaps it was an apparition, a vision like the ones he would see at the end of the tunnel of light—beckoning him through those painful nights of recovery. That light and the ethereal image at the end of it were the only things that gave him hope and the will to go on. He hadn't seen the vision since he'd left the military hospital in Afghanistan, until now.

But it wasn't his imagination and the image wasn't a result of hallucinations from the pain. She was real and she moved as if walking on air. The lightweight white clothing that she wore gently floated around her, lifted by the gentle breeze.

Maurice sat up a bit to see where she was going, and to convince himself that she was real. She turned a corner, and disappeared behind one of the houses. He stared at the space where she'd been until his vision blurred. He shook his head and blinked his eyes several times to clear them. The strange, unsettling sensation rippled in the center of his stomach.

"Crazy," he muttered to himself and tried to push the moment aside. He closed his eyes, leaned back and let the medication do its work. He dozed lightly and the one thing that he remembered when he awoke and found the sun setting down beyond the horizon was that he'd dreamed of the illuminated image again.

Chapter 4

"Are all the cabins full?" Layla asked, sipping on her mojito.

Desiree, her husband, Lincoln, and Layla were seated at the on-site bar relaxing and catching up while listening to the backdrop of soft jazz and calypso floating in from some unseen source.

"We have three vacancies, for now. But they're already booked. Of course everyone isn't staying for the entire season. The majority are here for about two weeks," Desiree said, then popped some peanuts into her mouth.

"Surprisingly, business has remained pretty good, even in the off-season," Lincoln said.

"During hard times people need some kind of escape, even if it's only temporary," Layla added.

"True, that's why we work really hard to keep the prices down and the service up," Desiree said. "And at least once every quarter we have a half-price weekend special with all amenities included."

"That must really help to draw in the business and make people want to come back."

"It does. And of course Melanie recommends all of her clients to come and visit. When she has functions up at her place and clients want to stay over, some of her guests will stay here."

"Can't wait to see Mel. I haven't seen her since the wedding," Layla said.

"She's out of town but she should be back early next week. She insisted on hosting our anniversary party, so I know she will have plenty to do when she gets back. And she has a long list of very eligible men she wants you to meet."

"Meeting men is not on my list of things to do. I came here to get away from the city, help you out and get some sun in. That's it."

Desiree and Lincoln shared a quick "sure you're right" look, between them.

Layla pushed out a breath and slowly gazed around at the tranquil setting. Singles and couples walked along the beach, gathered beneath umbrella covered tables or swam in the pool. Several guests were entering the restaurant and the sound of happy voices filled the air. She could easily get used to living like this. The whole notion of not having to think about where she was going to park her car every day was more than worth the price of admission.

"Did you show Layla her place?" Lincoln asked.

"Yes."

"Love it," Layla said. "I get the feeling that the two of you have intentions of me being around for a while." She looked from one guilty face to the other.

"We just want you to be happy and comfortable," Desiree offered, putting on her sweet as syrup voice.

Lincoln draped his arm around his wife's shoulder. "And if you decided to stay," he hedged, "you'd be all set up already. As a businessman I have to always think ahead."

Layla deadpanned the two of them and then laughed. "You two are a mess."

"We try," they said in unison.

"Listen," Lincoln pushed back from his seat. "I'm going to leave you ladies to do whatever it is that you do and I'm going to check on some inventory." He leaned over and gave his wife a slow, sweet kiss and whispered something against her lips that Layla couldn't make out, but whatever it was it had Desiree's face flushed with heat.

Desiree's gaze followed Lincoln until he was out of sight. She sighed deeply. A light smile softened her lips.

"You two are still as hot for each other as boiling oil."

"Is it that obvious?" Desiree teased. She reached for her glass of white wine.

"Uh, yeah."

The friends laughed.

"So when did you want me to start? Did you let your guests know about the new massage therapy services yet?"

"I've been working on a small flyer to hand out, but I wanted your input first to make sure I had all the details right and I wanted you to have a couple of days to unwind and relax."

"Girl, around here, I could get too relaxed and you wouldn't get any work out of me!"

"I know the feeling. But that's the kind of atmosphere Lincoln and I want at The Port. A real getaway, you know what I mean. If you look around, you don't see anyone hunched over laptops and checking BlackBerries and iPhones every five minutes. They're actually here to enjoy themselves. At least that's what I see when they come out of their rooms," she added as a caveat.

Layla nodded in agreement. "In that case," she raised her hand to get the attention of the bartender, "another mojito please."

Layla couldn't stay in bed a minute longer. And as much as she wanted to simply loll around on the sandy shores like a careless beach bum, the urge to be busy grabbed hold of her. She was actually anxious to get her massage room ready and her fingers moving. All night she'd dreamed of how she was going to set up her space and the atmosphere she would create. This would actually be the first time that a work space would truly be all hers and not the vision of whomever she was working for. A twinge of memory tried to pull her back to those times with Brent, with him teaching her the techniques that made her successful, that they practiced on each other late at night. She shook off the vision. That was the past she reminded herself once again.

It was barely seven a.m. and she was bathed and dressed. She tucked her iPad into her tote bag and headed out.

The morning was simply exquisite. The sun was at a perfect pitch. The sky was clear enough to see for miles and the gentle warmth that blew in from the ocean was invigorating. She spotted several guests jogging along the shoreline and there were already a few out for an early morning swim in the pale blue ocean.

Layla drew in a long breath and smiled. Whatever reservations she may have had about packing up and leaving the city were fading fast.

Desiree had given Layla the key to the massage suite the previous evening after their cursory tour. It was during the night that her wheels started spinning and she woke up knowing exactly what she wanted.

She let herself in and stood in the center of the

room and looked around. She took out her iPad and opened it to the Notepad icon and began jotting down a list of the things that she would need, from thick towels, to oils, literature on massage therapy, robes, slippers, lighting and music. She would also need cases of water and a place to keep them cold.

Lincoln and Desiree didn't cut corners on design layout or expense. Connected to the therapy room were shower stalls and a sauna room.

Layla guessed that what Desiree said was true; that if she didn't take this spot someone else would. And she would be right. It was perfect and she couldn't wait to get started.

She could already envision the space as a full-time operation with a staff. She grinned, knowing that she was getting way ahead of herself. The first thing she needed to do was make a list and then go shopping for supplies before she started reviewing resumes.

Layla switched off the lights and locked up, her mind on the task ahead as she came around the short corner and came face-to-face with Maurice Lawson.

She came up short, and started to apologize for nearly causing a collision, but the words hung somewhere in the back of her throat, stuck there with all the air that refused to move of out of her lungs and fuel her brain.

Her center ignited and she could feel the fine hairs on her arms and along the back of her neck begin to rise. Good Lord, the man was…was…

It was her. The woman that he'd spotted yesterday. She was real. "Sorry," he said.

The two-syllable word sounded like a love song in her ears.

"No, you're fine…it's fine. Really." *Did she just say that?* "I'm always in a hurry," she babbled. She couldn't think straight, not with those haunting dark eyes staring at her and that chiseled upper body encased in a sleeveless white T-shirt that outlined every muscle that begged to be touched.

Maurice shifted his walking cane from his right hand to his left and shook hers. "Maurice."

Her hand was enveloped in the warmth of his. "Nice…to meet you I mean. You're a guest?"

"Yes. You?"

"Yes and no. I'm a working guest. I'm the new massage therapist. Layla Brooks."

"Hmmm." He nodded his head.

They stood there momentarily frozen in that "what now" moment that was mercifully broken by another guest needing to squeeze by in the narrow corridor.

"Nice meeting you," Maurice said.

"You, too."

He moved past her and tried to ignore the pain in his leg and limped away with as much dignity as he could summon. He wanted to vanish and not have her watch him as he tried to pretend that he was as whole as any other man.

Layla didn't realize that she'd stopped breathing until a burst of air rushed from her chest. Her heart was beating triple time and although she was much too young for hot flashes, her entire body was flushed with heat.

"Humph, humph, humph. That is one specimen of a man, cane and all," she whispered. She definitely wanted him to sign up to be on her client list so that she could see for herself just how hard those muscles really were. She gave a short shake of her head to clear it.

It was still a little too early to drive into town. She took a slow stroll around the property, reacquainting herself with the layout and then around to the back of the main building to the outdoor lounge, drawn by the aroma of breakfast. Her stomach responded.

A few of the white circular tables were occupied and the waitresses were busy filling juice glasses and coffee cups. She found a table that was near the buffet, put down her bag and walked over to check out the breakfast offerings. She started down the length of the table and filled her plate with fresh fruit, eggs and wheat toast. She walked back to her table and was thinking about her close encounter with tall, dark and handsome Maurice when the plate in her hand rattled. He was on the other side of the buffet table.

Maurice was settling down in his seat. Alone. He braced his cane against the table and she could see from where she stood the relief wash over his expression as he took the weight off of his leg.

She wondered what had happened to him. Was it an accident? Surgery? She watched the expression on his face tighten. For a moment he closed his eyes while he massaged his thigh. What would that thigh feel like under her expert fingers? She knew she could take the pain away.

"Um, excuse me."

Layla blinked. A smile flickered across her mouth. "Oh, sorry. I'm daydreaming," she said to the couple standing behind her that was waiting for her to move along. She walked with her plate back to her table, taking furtive glances in Maurice's direction.

He was reading the paper and sipping on a cup of coffee. Maybe she should go and join him. No sense in the both of them eating alone, she thought. A dozen different scenarios played in her head on how she should approach him and what she should say and what he would say to her in return. The minutes ticked away.

Maurice put down his coffee cup and turned slightly in her direction then away before doing a short double take and looking back again. He lifted his chin in salute. Layla waved. Her heart pounded. Maybe he would come over. Maybe he would ask her to join him. Should she go over and sit down? What if he was waiting for someone and she looked silly?

Maurice folded the paper, finished off his coffee and reached for his cane.

He was going to come over. She could hardly breathe. She swallowed over the tightness in her throat.

Maurice stood slowly offered her a brief smile and walked out.

Layla felt as if she'd been pumped full of air and then suddenly stabbed with an ice pick. As the air in her balloon dissipated, so did her appetite. She pushed her food around on her plate until it was sufficiently cold then gathered up her things and went out to get her car for the drive into town.

Maurice returned to his room. He'd wanted to say something more to Layla. But what was the point. He tossed his cane into a corner. He plopped down on the couch. Even if he was attracted to her, what would she want with him? She probably felt pity for him just like everyone else.

He stretched out his injured leg and absently massaged the never-ending ache.

It had been longer than he would have liked since he'd been with a woman, through choice as well as circumstance. After his injury and then rehab he continued to struggle with what happened that night. The guilt was almost as painful if not more so than the injury that ended his career. The therapy sessions helped, but only so much. He still could not get beyond the feeling that had he done something differently, lives would have been saved and he would be one hundred percent man. Without his career as a Navy SEAL, the job he'd worked so hard for, trained for, lived for—all of that was gone. Being a SEAL defined who he was. The loss of that combined with his debilitating injury was almost more than he could stand. He didn't feel like a man anymore. And if he didn't feel it, what woman would feel it? He leaned his head back against the cushion of the couch and closed his eyes against his incscapable realities.

Layla spent the better part of the morning shopping for supplies for the suite. Her car's trunk was loaded and it took several trips back and forth to unload and get everything inside the suite. She'd purchased plants, artwork, oils, lotions, CDs, mats, small bowls, oil burners, hand sanitizers, disinfectant, cases of fruit juice and water, and soft lightbulbs. She'd placed an order for a dozen terry cloth robes and shower slippers. The boutique where she'd made her purchases promised that her items would be delivered within the next two days.

She spent the next couple of hours organizing her supplies and rolling towels to be stacked. She hung pictures and poured the aromatic oils into the burners. Aromatherapy was just as important in creating the perfect atmosphere as the treatments.

Layla took a look around and was finally satisfied with what she'd accomplished. She took some pictures of the space for the flyers, then locked up and walked back to the main building in search of Desiree.

"It looks fabulous," Desiree was saying. "Let me download them to my computer."

Layla touched a few icons on her iPad and sent the images to Desiree.

Within moments Desiree was loading them into her graphics program. "You've been busy," she said while she worked.

Layla laughed. "To keep my mind off of other things."

Desiree looked up at her friend for a moment. "Other things like what? Don't tell me New York."

Layla sat on the edge of Desiree's desk and folded her arms. "No. Not New York." She leaned closer. "Do you know that guy…with the limp?"

Desiree frowned in concentration. "Limp?"

"Yes and gorgeous."

Desiree grinned. "Oh, Maurice Lawson."

"Him."

Desiree crossed her legs. Her right brow rose with her question. "What about him?"

"What do you know about him?"

"Hmm, not much. He checked in about three days ago. Booked his cottage for six weeks. That's about it really. I see him around from time to time." A slow smile moved across her mouth. "And you want to know all this because…"

Layla blew out a breath. "I wish I knew. Well,

maybe I do know. It's hard to explain. I mean, I only saw him for a minute a couple of times…but…" She looked away as if searching for the answers somewhere in the corners of the room. Finally, she shrugged. "No big deal. Forget it. He looked like he'd rather be alone."

Desiree stared at Layla's profile. "Hey, this is the twenty-first century, girl. If a woman is interested in a man she doesn't have to stand on protocol and wait for the man to make the first move anymore."

Layla slowly shook her head. "That is so not me. In my head I'm bold and aggressive. But then reality sets in."

Desiree reached out and touched Layla's hand. "Bold and not standing on protocol *is* you. Brent screwed up a perfectly good relationship. But you can't let what he did diminish you. Every man is not like Brent."

Layla hopped down off the desk. "I know that. I'm over Brent."

"Arc you? Really? I'm not saying that you still have feelings for him, but I am saying that what he did messed with your confidence, challenged your womanhood."

Layla snapped her head away. She tightened her arms around her waist. The words to refute Desiree's assertion were on her lips. They lingered on her tongue. She couldn't say them. What Desiree said was true. It was painfully true. It had been a year since she'd come home to have him tell her that he was leaving, that he no longer loved her. But there wasn't a day that had gone by that she didn't remember how small and insignificant she'd felt; how could he so easily stop loving her. It wasn't until months later that she found out why.

She'd gone over that night a million times. In some versions she threw a lamp at Brent and then dumped all of his clothes out of the window. In another he came running after her, begging her to forgive him. But in all the versions, in the end, she was alone. Probably what stung the most was that she'd heard from their mutual acquaintances that Brent and Grace—his assistant—the woman he'd stopped loving her for—were still together and there was talk of *them* getting married the following spring.

There was no way that she could get around the feeling that it was something she'd done or didn't do or that she wasn't appealing enough. *Something*. The feeling of inadequacy was not as bad as it had been, but it hovered and sat on her shoulder waiting patiently to whisper in her ear.

"I remember the Layla Brooks that would walk into a minefield with high heels and a smile on her face, who could step into a room and every head would turn, who could have a conversation with the Secretary of State as easily as the woman who owns the dry cleaner on the corner. *That's* the Layla that I know."

Layla lowered her head for a moment. Had she really changed that much? She looked at Desiree. "So I should just walk up to him and what?"

"Hand him one of your flyers for starters," she said pressing the print button on the computer. Moments later a color-printed flyer announcing the new massage therapy services slid out of the printer. Desiree lifted it from the tray and handed it to Layla with a "now what's your excuse," look on her face.

Layla tilted her head slightly to the left and eyed the flyer. "Not bad. I'll see what I can do with it," she said with a lift of her chin before turning away and waving goodbye on her way out.

Chapter 5

Layla made it a point to be on the lookout for Maurice, but it had been three days since she'd seen him last. Desiree assured her that he hadn't checked out. Maybe they simply kept missing each other, she'd suggested. Or maybe it just wasn't meant to be, Layla concluded.

Whatever the case may be, her massage services were officially open for business and from the moment she turned on the lights, she was busy and she didn't have much time to dwell on the illusive Maurice Lawson.

The nightmares had begun again. He awoke that morning with his entire body aching, damp from sweat and his head pounding. The dark, twisted images began to recede as the sun rose over the horizon, but the feeling of helplessness lingered. He'd been caught in the clutches of his deepest fears for hours, listening to the explosions and the screams and the heat from the flames that seemed to go on into infinity. He couldn't get away because he couldn't wake up until a soft glow could be seen in the valley of the dark mountains where his Black Hawk had gone down. It beckoned him, getting brighter when he seemed to lose his way. He could feel the bands of darkness that held him down begin to loosen as the light grew brighter. It felt as if he was being lifted from a deep pit. And then he woke up.

For a while he simply lay in bed and stared at the ceiling and watched the blades of the fan turn in slow, hypnotic circles.

Would it ever end? Would he ever feel whole again? Some days it almost seemed possible and then there were others, like today that had him believing that this endless dark road was his future. But it couldn't be. He couldn't live like this day after day. He would go out of his mind.

He sat up in bed. His T-shirt clung to his upper body. Gingerly he eased his legs over the side and closed his eyes for a moment as the pain dimmed enough for him to think about getting up. With some effort he pushed himself to a standing position, took a deep breath and limped into the bathroom.

Even after a long hot shower, the pulsing aches in his body persisted, beating like his heart. He took his time getting dressed and finally stepped outside onto the front porch of the cottage.

Another magnificent day. The sky was clear for miles. The air hinted at the summer just beyond the horizon. The sun was at that perfect angle. Faint sounds of laughter and life could be heard in the distance. He should be enjoying it. He should be diving into the ocean or jogging along the sandy beach, lounging with friends in the late afternoon, sipping drinks with island names and sleeping with his arms wrapped around a beautiful woman at night.

He drew in a long breath as he leaned against the pillar that supported the overhang. The caw of seagulls wafted in the breeze. He turned his attention to the path leading to the main building and wondered if the woman he'd met—Layla—had opened her massage spa yet. The idea of her hands on his body stroking away the tightness, releasing the tension that coiled in his limbs and down his spine, caused an inadvertent moan to escape. He imagined the pressure of her fingers playing across his neck, massaging his biceps. Her scent filled his nostrils and the sudden tug in his groin heated his blood.

He shook his head to clear the cobwebs of lust that had ensnared him. It was as if she'd cast some kind of spell over him. From the moment he'd caught sight of her walking along the pathway, he'd been unable to shake her from his thoughts.

It was *her* image, *her* light that finally led him out of the grip of his nightmare. Although he could not see her in his dream, he understood that it was her. How, he was not certain. But he felt it in the depths of his being.

Layla had been open for business since nine a.m. It was nearing one o'clock and she'd been going nonstop. Although she loved what she did, she knew she couldn't keep up the pace and still maintain her high standards of quality. As soon as she shut down for the day, she was going to have to take some time and plan a schedule that was going to work for her and not shortchange the guests.

She'd put the "Out to Lunch" sign on the door and was in the middle of resetting the massage room when there was a knock on the front door.

"Go away," she muttered under her breath as she rolled a fresh towel and put it on the shelf. She picked up the basket of used towels and walked to the front. "Whoever it is obviously cannot—"

Her throat went dry. She went to the glass door and turned the lock.

"Hi."

"Hi. Uh, sorry to disturb your lunch…but I wanted to make an appointment."

She couldn't stop watching the movement of his mouth and the way his lips reminded her of summer fruit—sweet and juicy. Too bad she didn't read lips because she had no idea what he'd just said.

"I probably should come back," he said when he got no response. He started to turn away.

She reached out and touched his arm. Big mistake. It was like being hit with a jolt of electricity. Her breath hitched for an instant. "No…you have to excuse my rudeness. Please come in. I guess I'm a little tired and not thinking clearly." She held the door open wider and smiled up at him. "Come in."

Maurice looked at her for a moment then stepped past her and inside.

She allowed herself an instant of mental happy dancing before she closed the door and followed him to the middle of the waiting lounge.

"Please, have a seat." She extended her hand toward one of the mauve-print club chairs.

"It's easier if I stand."

"Hmm, okay. So…what can I do for you?" She rested her hip against the side of the reception desk.

"I was interested in what you offer…your services."

Her throat went bone-dry. *He had the longest lashes.* Were those flecks of cinnamon in his eyes? Every time that he said something the rich timbre of his voice vibrated inside her like a tuning fork.

She ran her tongue across her lips. "Umm, I could show you around, give you the ten cent tour. I'm sorry that I haven't had brochures made up yet, but the list of services are posted on the wall."

He turned slightly to the left and glimpsed the whiteboard with the list. Slowly, he walked over, trying to minimize his limp. "You do all of this?" He turned his head toward her and his eyes seemed to sparkle above his yummy smile.

"Yep." She stuck her hands out and wiggled her fingers.

His laughter filled her with a wild sense of gleeful abandonment. "Take your pick."

"What would you suggest?"

She crossed the short space to stand next to him and folded her arms. She scanned the board and made a mental note that she reached his shoulder. "Hmm, I would start you off with a steam for ten minutes, followed by a full-body massage and some aromatherapy."

He angled toward her and glanced down into her upturned face. She seemed to be lit from within. A warmth radiated from her and embraced him in a soothing cocoon. He felt…peaceful. That was it. She took all the noise away.

Maurice cleared his throat. "I know you're probably booked." His dark, smoky eyes rolled slowly over her face, down the long column of her neck and…

"I have an opening…" She coughed into her fist. "'Scuse me." Her face was on fire. "At the end of the day. If five o'clock works for you." She swallowed and wondered if he could actually hear her heart hammering in her chest.

"Five is fine. Do I need to bring anything?"

"No." She offered a smile. "Just yourself."

He grinned at her and she noticed the small dimple in his right cheek.

"See you at five."

She probably should have run over and opened the door for him or something, but she just stood there like Lot's wife—a pillar of salt.

She snapped out of it when the chime over the door signaled his departure and she actually breathed in and out. She sat down on the side of the desk and stared at the empty space that Maurice had filled moments ago. What the hell was it about that man that made her all un-Layla? She knew the pitfalls of sexual magnetism that drowned out everything else. Because what else could it be but a crazy sexual attraction? He was a stranger albeit a tall, dark, gorgeous stranger that had her libido on overdrive. Meanwhile, the man only wanted a massage, not a long, lusty, sweaty roll in the sack.

She shook her head and pushed up from the side of the desk. "Yeah, it's been too long since you've had a man."

The next four hours crept by. In between each application of oil, or deep tissue pressure onto the backs and thighs of her clients, Layla checked the clock. Was it really possible what they said about time standing still?

Mercifully her last client walked out of the door. It was 4:30. The speed of her heart began a steady spiral. She busied herself with reorganizing, restocking and making sure that the perfect combination of oils were on hand. She lit two of the oil burners in the massage room and within moments the dimly lit room was awash in a heady, soothing scent of ylang-ylang.

At precisely five on the dot, the chimes over the door jingled. She drew in a breath and walked out front.

Her spirit dropped to her ankles but she still plastered a welcoming smile on her face.

"Hello, how may I help you?" she asked the young blonde woman who stood in the door looking very much like Reese Witherspoon.

"Hi. I wanted to find out about the services."

"Sure. Let me show you the list of what I offer." They walked over to the whiteboard and Layla began explaining the services.

"Pretty extensive."

"I want this to be as full-service as I can manage," Layla said with a smile. "What brings you to The Port?"

The woman took off her dark shades to reveal startling green eyes. "Needed to get away. I lost my husband a little more than a year ago. This time of year is very difficult." She forced a tight smile. "I hoped with a change in location…it might be easier."

"Oh, I'm so sorry."

She waved off the remark. "Thank you. I'm sure you don't need to hear my sad story."

The door chimed again. Layla's gaze snapped in the direction of the opening door. Maurice stood in the frame of the doorway and she felt all the alarms go off at once.

The woman glanced over her shoulder wondering who or what had caused Layla to stop talking midsentence.

Layla's breath hitched for an instant. "Hello."

The woman's gaze moved between Layla and Maurice. She put her shades back on. "Do you have a card?"

Layla blinked. "Oh, yes. Of course." She hurried over to her desk and retrieved a card from the silver plated holder and handed it to the woman.

"How far in advance do I need to make an appointment?"

"You can always call when you're ready. If I have an opening I'll be happy to immediately accommodate you. But if you want an appointment if you can call at least the day before, I can usually work something out. It's been pretty busy since I've opened."

The woman nodded. "Thank you for your time. I'm sure you'll be hearing from me." She extended her hand. "My name is Kim by the way."

"Hope to see you again, Kim."

Kim walked toward the door. She gave a slight nod of her head and started to walk out but then stopped. She frowned just a bit as she looked up at Maurice as if trying to get him into focus. "You look familiar. I know it's a big world, but are you any relation to Rafe Lawson?"

Layla noticed the subtle tightening of his expression.

"Cousin."

Kim beamed and wagged her finger. "I knew I spotted a resemblance." She stuck out her hand. "Kim Fleming. I haven't seen Rafe in ages. Please tell him hello for me."

"Sure."

She opened the door. "Thanks again," she said to Layla. "You two have a good afternoon." She offered a knowing smile and walked out.

Layla folded her hands in front of her. "Small world, huh?"

"Yeah," he murmured. "Listen maybe we can do this another time."

He finally focused on her and the raw anger that was reflected in his eyes and the set countenance of his face caused Layla to take an inadvertent step back. His thick brows were drawn tightly together and his full mouth had tightened into a flat line. His chest rose and fell much too rapidly.

Layla's eyes moved over his face and down to his

hand that clenched the handle of his cane in a death grip. She dared to reach out. She covered that hand with her own.

"I can guarantee that after an hour whatever it is that's bothering you won't seem quite as important," she said softly.

Maurice's gaze dropped down to their hands then slowly up to her face. By degrees the knot in his gut began to loosen. He rocked his jaw from side to side. The corner of his mouth lifted ever so slightly. "You must be *very* good."

She grinned full out. "I am." She propped her hands on her hips. "And if you are not one hundred percent satisfied…dinner is on me."

Maurice laughed from deep in his chest. The corner of his eyes crinkled. "You're on."

"And I promise not to gloat over how incredible you will feel when I'm done."

She turned to lead him to the changing room.

"If you're that good, then dinner *and* drinks will be on me."

She nearly stumbled over her own two feet but had the presence of mind to keep walking. "Mojito is my drink of choice," she said and tossed him a quick look over her shoulder.

Maurice chuckled and followed willingly in her wake.

Chapter 6

"You can change in here," Layla said, opening a door to a small changing space that included a locker, a bench for sitting and a hook for hanging clothes. "It's not the Ritz but it's cozy," she added with a smile.

Maurice offered a half grin. "It's more than fine. Thanks."

"When you're done, walk straight down this short hall to the steam room." She indicated the direction to her right. "I'll have it all set up for you." She turned and the saloon door swung closed behind her. As she walked toward the steam room all she could think about was that gorgeous man was in the process of taking off his clothes, and the next time that

she set eyes on him, there would be not much between them other than a white towel…*of surrender*,
her sex-starved brain whispered. Goose bumps shimmied up her arms.

Layla shook off the tempting visual and hurried
into the steam room that housed three spaces for clients. She selected the room on the end and set the
temperature, made sure that there were towels and
water. She came out and shut the door behind her.
When she turned Maurice was standing in front of
her and they both heard her gasp.

"Sorry, I didn't mean to startle you."

She ran her tongue nervously across her lips. "It's
nothing…really. Just a little jumpy today for some
reason." In a nanosecond her gaze licked across his
face to his muscular bare chest, to the tight stomach, to the hidden gems behind the white towel and
down to his legs and back up again. She swallowed.
"Your room is ready."

"Thanks."

"You can adjust the temperature if you need to.
Everything is set for ten minutes. Press the red button on the wall and the steam will start."

He nodded his head.

She took two steps back. "Shout if you need me…
for anything."

"I will." His eyes crinkled in the corners when
he smiled at her.

"Okay. Good." She took two more back steps then

spun away before she really made an idiot out of herself. She had the clarity of mind to point herself in the direction of the massage room. Once inside she sat down on the low-slung chair and dropped her face into her palms. What in the world was wrong with her? Her entire self was behaving as if she'd never been in the presence of a sexy man before. She couldn't think straight, her heart was racing a mile a minute, and every other word out of her mouth was laced with a sexual undertone. Pushing out an exasperated breath she stood and began preparing the room for her client. This was business, she continued to remind herself as she set out towels, an extra robe, and lit the oil burners to scent the room. She put on a CD that captured the hypnotic sounds of rainfall and the rush of waves against the shore. She checked her watch. Maurice had about three minutes. She dimmed the lighting and went to check on her client.

When she returned to the steam room, Maurice was already out. She could hear the shower water running and her imagination shifted into overdrive. As clear as a spring morning she could see him beyond the frosted glass doors in the outfit that the Lord had given him…long, hard, sleek and drenched in milk chocolate.

The rushing water of the shower stopped. She could clearly hear him humming a soft tune now. Her heart thumped. She couldn't just stand there like a dummy. *But what if he came out with nothing on for instance? Not even the towel.* But her feet were stuck on the wood floors.

The frosted glass door swung open. Maurice was securing the towel around his waist. He glanced up. His entire body still glistened from the heat and the water and for a moment Layla refused to breathe, certain that if she did it would disturb the delicate balance between them.

"Oh, hey there. All done." He used the end of the towel that was draped around his neck to wipe his face.

Layla pushed out a breath. "Great. We can get your massage started." She turned on her heels and walked back in the direction of the massage room. She could feel the heat of Maurice's body wrapping itself around her from behind. The massage room was up ahead. She opened the door and stepped into the dimly lit interior. Immediately she busied herself with arranging oils and cloths. Anything to keep her eyes off of Maurice.

"Is the room comfortable enough?"

"Fine."

"You can get up on the table. If you loosen the towel and turn on your stomach we can get started." She looked away as he loosened his towel and then stretched out on the massage table.

Layla walked around to the head of the table. "I want to make sure that you're comfortable. Stretch your arms down your sides, palms up and rest your forehead in the opening of the headrest. Get comfortable."

Maurice followed her instructions. "Good?" he asked, his voice muffled by the cushion of the head support.

"Perfect. I'm going to begin with a light full-body massage and then a deeper tissue stimulation. I'll be using a variety of oils. If I'm applying too much pressure or you feel uncomfortable please let me know. If there is an area on your body that you want me to devote special attention, let me know that as well."

"Hmm, ummm," he mumbled.

Layla poured some oil onto her palm and rubbed her hands briskly together. For a moment she closed her eyes and drew in a deep breath. Slowly she lowered her hands to his shoulders. Her hands splayed across the heat of his flesh. Her thumbs pressed and connected with hard muscle, and his rugged sigh made her own spine tingle. She forced herself to concentrate on what she did so well—bring heaven to earth through her touch.

She covered every exposed inch of his body with her hands, infusing into every sinew the heat of release. Her trained hands moved down his back, up again and across his wide shoulders. She kneaded his arms, and she'd swear that she heard him almost whimper in rapture when she stroked the inside of his palms.

Applying more oils onto her hands, she started

on the odyssey of his upper thighs and then took a slow trip down along his calves to the soles of his feet and back up again. She lingered for a moment along the thick scar that ran like a river down his right leg from above his knee to his midcalf. She felt his body tighten and his easy breathing hitch when her fingertips came in contact with the thickened tissue. But under her gentle manipulations she heard his breathing level off and the tension dissipate.

The soft candlelight bounced off his glistening dark skin, casting enticing shadows along the dips and curves of his body. Layla drew in a slow breath separating his natural scent from that of the oils. A smile of satisfaction teased her mouth.

She let her lids lower to almost closing as she worked. She loved what she did, bringing pleasure and relief to others through the skill of her touch. But this was different. She'd always been able to remain detached from her clients. She simply read their body needs through the tips of her fingers and gave the body what it desired. But this time it was *her* body that was in need, *her* body that longed to be touched.

Without effort or apparent intent Maurice had awakened her sleeping sexual giant. And it needed to be fed. The pulse between her thighs quickened. A fire lit in her belly. Heat infused her. Her breathing escalated. She saw herself standing before him. Her robe dropped to the ground. She stretched out her arms. He came to her in the dimness. His mouth brushed the pulse that fluttered at the base of her neck. Her nostrils flared as she tried to breathe. His head moved lower down along the swell of her breasts...

Maurice groaned every so softly.

The sound rippled up her spine. She blinked. Her chest rose and fell in rapid succession. She ran her tongue across her dry mouth.

The room came into a hazy kind of focus. *Damn,* she muttered under her breath. She glanced down at the sculpted specimen beneath her fingers.

"All done," she said softly. "How do you feel?"

"Like I could stay here forever."

Layla expelled a nervous laugh. "There's a robe hanging on the back of the door. After you get your things and get dressed I'll meet you up front."

"Hmmm," he murmured unmoving.

Layla slipped out, closing the door silently behind her.

There was one thing that Maurice was totally thankful for, he thought, slowly rising to a sitting position on the table, and that was that she hadn't asked him to turn over onto his back. He glanced down at the rock-hard rise beneath the towel. That could have been embarrassing for both of them. Or maybe not.

While she ran her hands all over him he was able to forget that he wasn't whole—forget that he was crippled and scarred. Under the expertise of Layla's fingertips he felt complete, came alive again, things he had not felt since he woke up in the hospital more than a year ago.

Gingerly he got down off of the table, expecting the usual pain to shoot up his leg into his hip. But nothing happened. All he felt was a soothing warmth deep in his muscles. He took a step and still no real pain. He reached for the robe that hung on the hook and shrugged into it. He took a quick mental inventory of his body. A hint of a smile moved his mouth. It didn't hurt. He didn't hurt. His throat clenched and his eyes burned. He didn't care if the relief only lasted for a minute. But for right now...

Layla was sitting in front of the computer screen when Maurice came up front.

She stopped what she was doing. "So...how was it? Can I add you to my list of satisfied customers?"

He crossed the space and sat down on a stool in front of the desk. "Oh, most definitely." He grinned.

Layla tried to stay focused on whatever it was she should say next rather than memorize the way his lips moved when he talked and wonder if they were as soft and sweet as they appeared.

"Looks like I owe you a drink and dinner."

She laughed over her nerves and waved her hand. "Oh, that's not necessary."

"A deal is a deal."

Layla didn't breathe for a second. "Drinks and dinner?"

"Mojito, right?" His eyes glowed.

"Um, yes."

"How about eight?"

She swallowed the last lump of hesitation. "Eight is fine. I can meet you…by the bar."

Maurice bobbed his head. "See you later." He started to turn then stopped. "Thank you."

"You're more than welcome."

Layla sat transfixed until the sound of the chimes over the door signaled Maurice's departure. She shook some sense back into her head. She tugged on her bottom lip with her teeth. Dinner with Maurice Lawson! She had a little more than an hour to get ready and it would never happen with her sitting there with a goofy grin on her face.

And maybe over dinner and after a drink or two he would tell her a little bit about his very famous family and why that woman's mentioning them seemed to get under his skin.

Chapter 7

"Hey, Layla!"

Layla glanced over her shoulder to see Desiree hurrying in her direction. "Hey. Whatsup?" she asked barely slowing down.

"I wanted to know how your day went and if you wanted to join me and Lincoln for dinner."

"Oh," she stopped short, turned to look at Desiree with a grin on her face. "I'm having dinner with Maurice Lawson."

Desiree's brows shot up in perfect symmetry. "Mr. tall, dark and broodingly handsome?"

"Yep."

"Get outta here. You must have put some of that massage mojo on the brother. I haven't seen him with a soul since he's been here. To be truthful other than spotting him alone on the beach or maybe grabbing a drink…" Her voice trailed off.

"Did you know that he was a Lawson cousin?"

Desiree frowned. "No, I didn't, but I see that you do," she added with a wry grin. "How did you find out?"

They reached the end to the path before it split up toward the cottages.

"One of your guests, Kim Fleming, came into the salon while he was there. She recognized the family resemblance. Of course she mentioned Rafe."

Desiree laughed. "Who doesn't mention Rafe if they know him?"

"Touché. Anyway, it seemed to upset him for some reason."

"Hmmm, I could probably ask Melanie. She would know. She's close with the Lawsons. Funny, I never put the family thing together. Like I said, I haven't really seen him that much and one of the staff checked him in. But even from a distance I can tell that the man is fine—with a capital *F*."

Layla laughed. "You are so right." She checked her watch. "I gotta run. We're meeting up at eight."

"Do you, girl. We'll catch up later. And have fun tonight. You deserve it."

"Thanks." She hurried along the path and around the short bend to her cottage.

Layla tossed her tote bag on the club chair in her

bedroom and then darted into the bathroom to get the shower going while she figured out what she was going to wear. Something simple, but classy and definitely not too sexy, she mused as she sifted through her very sparse wardrobe. When she'd finally decided to come to Sag Harbor for the summer, her thoughts had been wrapped around getting out of the city, being in a beach environment, i.e., shorts and T-shirts, and working at the salon. In other words, her wardrobe lacked that "date night ready appeal."

Sighing, she finally settled on a pair of chocolate-colored capri pants and a draped neck sleeveless top in the same shade. She did have the presence of mind to pack a few accessories. She found her multi-strand silver chain necklace to add another dimension to the chocolate soufflé colors she had going on and she added her novelty bracelets. With that major chore out of the way, she darted into the bathroom for a quick shower.

Maurice sat at the bar, sipping on a glass of bourbon on the rocks. This was a mistake. He knew that she only said yes because she was being nice and felt sorry for him. He sipped his drink. He winced as the throb pulsed in his thigh—building like a storm on the horizon. His hand shook ever so slightly. It was too good to be true—the two hours of freedom from his hell. He needed to get back to his room and take his pain medicine before it got too bad. If that happened there would be nothing the little white pills could do for him. He'd have to go to the hospital for morphine.

He placed a ten dollar bill on the bar and turned on his stool. He pushed himself up, shut his eyes for an instant and gritted his teeth against the growing agony. When he opened them Layla was standing right in front of him.

"Hey," she said softly, immediately seeing the expression of agony on his face and sensing the physical discomfort he was in. Beads of perspiration dotted his hairline. She took his arm. "Let's sit at that table." She slid an arm around his waist and held him securely, forcing him to allow her to take some of his weight.

They made it over to the table and Maurice managed to slide onto the banquet seating. Layla scooted in next to him and told him to take deep breaths in that throaty, hypnotic voice of hers.

"Slow and easy," she coaxed before placing her hands on his upper thigh.

Maurice flinched. "What—"

"Sssh, just relax and breathe," she said with a smile, "or you'll have everyone thinking I'm doing something kinky under the table."

He managed a laugh through his grimace.

The heat from her palms radiated through the fabric of his slacks and seeped beneath the surface of his flesh to the epicenter of his pain. The soothing warmth emanating from her hands was a magic balm. The throbbing was still present but the intensity had dwindled. She applied just the slightest amount of pressure while she reminded him to breathe slowly and deeply.

She watched that tight, pinched expression on his face begin to relax. The grip he had on the edge of the table loosened and the rapid pulse beat at his temple began to return to normal.

"Whatever, you're doing under that table," he turned and looked at her with such heat in his eyes that the muscles in her stomach quivered. "Don't stop. At least not anytime soon." He groaned in relief.

Layla blinked rapidly. She knew he was in pain. Her hands were trained to soothe pain. But she also knew what touching him did to her. It was making her wet and that was crazy. "Better?" she breathed.

Maurice nodded slowly. "Much. Thank you. Really."

"Don't mention it. I may have to refund your credit card. The therapy should have lasted more than two hours," she said, trying to make her voice sound light and noncommittal while her heart thudded. She linked her fingers together on top of the table and tried not to notice how long and thick his lashes were.

"No refunds. To be honest, the last couple of hours have been the best in more than a year."

She studied his carved profile—perfect angles and strong lines. He reached for his drink and took a swallow. She watched the warm brown liquid trail down his throat.

Maurice set his glass down and turned those maple brown eyes with flecks of cinnamon on her. "You want to order a drink or something first?"

"Sure."

Maurice raised his hand to get the waitress's attention.

"What can I get for you tonight?" She placed a menu in front of each of them.

Layla looked up at the young waitress. "A mojito."

"Right away. Can I get you a refill, sir?"

"No. Thanks. I'm good for a while. Give us a minute to look over the menu."

She bobbed her head. "Be right back with your drink."

Layla turned, taking in the room before studying the menu. She looked everywhere but at Maurice. Where all of her bravado of moments ago had gone was a mystery to her. Now she was brain dead and all thumbs. She couldn't think of one thing to say and for the life of her she couldn't make out a word on the menu. Every time she was around him, she got all nutty. Mercifully the waitress returned with her drink. It was barely on the table before she took a long sip.

Maurice chuckled. "Thirsty?"

Layla sputtered. "You noticed, huh?"

"I've been trained to notice things." His steady gaze rattled hers.

Layla zeroed in on her drink for a moment, regained her composure then asked him what kind of training.

It was his turn to hesitate. "Special Operations." His jaw clenched.

"What branch?"

"Navy. SEALs."

Her heart tripped. *A Navy SEAL.* "Oh. How long?" She brought the glass to her lips and took a short sip.

"Ten years." He slowly turned his glass in a small circle on the table.

"You must have seen the world."

His mouth warmed into a smile. "That I have. Not the way most people do, but I've seen my share."

Layla leaned forward. "Tell me about it," she said softly.

He looked at her. "Naw." He shook his head in refusal. "You don't want to hear all that macho testosterone stuff."

She poked his rock-hard biceps with the tip of her finger. "Yes, I do. Don't try to get out of it."

His long lashes fanned over his eyes several times before he spoke. He pushed out a breath and looked slightly away. "The first year was hard, grueling, mind and body altering training." He shook his head. "There were nights I would fall out from exhaustion and wonder what the hell I was doing. Then I'd get up and do it all over again." He finished off his drink. "It's dangerous work. It's honorable and only the best of the best make it and get the SEAL pin."

"What little I've heard about the Navy SEALs was always connected to some secret clandestine operation."

His eyes moved slowly across her face. "We get brought in when the stakes are very high and special tactical skills are needed to achieve a mission's success."

Layla was sure she knew what he meant. It was simply the way he said the words, the way his voice dipped down and stirred her center.

"Ready to order?"

Layla dragged her gaze away from Maurice and looked up at the waitress. It took a moment for her to put together in her head what the woman was saying.

"What do you recommend?" Maurice asked the waitress, but his focus was on Layla.

"The chef prepared an incredible lobster bisque that I would highly recommend as a starter."

"Sounds wonderful," Layla said needing to say something to distract her from the way Maurice was looking at her. Her body flushed with heat.

"Make that two."

The young woman nodded. "For your main course?" She looked from one to the other.

"I'll let the lady decide." He wrapped his long fingers around his glass.

"The, uh, grilled salmon salad sounds good."

"It is."

"Make that two," Maurice said again.

"I'll be back in a few moments."

Layla cleared her throat and glanced around. Why did she feel so unlike herself when she was around him? One minute she felt confident and secure and then he would look at her or there'd be something deep and dark in his voice and the earth would shift under her feet. "You were telling me about being a Navy SEAL. Where are some of the places you've been?"

His expression darkened. She watched his jaw set as if doused in cement. "Let's talk about something else. You. How did you wind up here giving massages?"

Layla leaned back a bit in her seat, willing herself to relax, thrown off once again by the sudden shift in his demeanor. "Well," she said on a breath, "Desiree is my soror. She's been asking me to come out for a while and I'd been putting it off."

"Why?"

She was surprised by his question. "Um, I... thought I had more important things to do in New York."

"Like what?"

She blinked, not sure how to answer, how much to tell him about her life. She went with the basics. "Work, friends…"

"Anyone special?"

Inwardly she flinched. But the soft sincerity of his tone took away the sting. She reached for her drink.

"You don't have to answer that."

"There was someone," she blurted out, surprising herself with the painful admission.

Maurice waited for more. Briefly he wondered if her hands made that *someone* feel the way that she made him feel. Or maybe it was the other way around. He reached for his now empty glass and wished that he'd ordered another one earlier.

Why was he looking at her as if he wanted to bore straight into her past and scoop it out? Layla cleared her throat. "Didn't work out," she managed. She brought her glass to her lips.

"His loss."

His luscious lips curved into a half grin and her legs involuntarily opened. Her knee brushed his. The jolt from the contact had her dribbling her drink over her bottom lip. She would have laughed but that would have made it worst. She reached for a napkin and quickly dabbed her lips.

The waitress returned with their soups.

"Enjoy," she said, placing one bowl in front of each of them. "Would you like me to refresh your drink, sir?"

"Yes, please."

She offered a short nod of her head and left them to their meal.

Maurice spread the cloth napkin on his lap. "You were telling me about the man you left behind."

"I'm pretty sure I wasn't saying all that."

"Something *like* that."

"Actually I wasn't telling you anything about him at all, other than it didn't work out." She dipped her spoon into her soup and lifted it to her mouth. "Oh… this is incredible."

"Hmmm, yes it is."

Layla glanced at him through her lashes. He was staring at her and he hadn't tasted his soup yet. *He was talking about her.* The realization sent a tingle right down her spine.

She cleared her throat. "How's your leg feeling?"

Maurice's dark gaze leapt to Layla's questioning face. He nodded slowly. "Bearable."

"How long?" she asked gently.

"Year and a half." He spooned the bisque into his mouth and avoided her stare.

She wanted to know more, but she could see the return of the set of his jaw and the deepening furrow of his brow. It was really none of her business anyway.

Maurice finished off his soup and pushed his bowl aside. He wiped his lips with the cloth napkin and set it neatly beside his bowl. The waitress returned with his drink. He thanked her with a brief nod and took a long swallow. His eyes briefly closed against the warm burn.

Layla watched every move—his economy of motion, even with the simplest of maneuvers. There was a purpose and precision with everything that he did. No excess. No extra. Fleetingly she wondered if he ever let go and what it would be like if he did. All that pent-up maleness released. The muscles in the bottom of her stomach curled deliciously in response to the possibility.

"So…you're related to the Lawsons. I've met—"

"I won't talk about my family."

The hard impact of his words was as precise as a missile. The target was the center of her chest.

"I'm sorry. I—"

His upheld hand stopped her mid-sentence. "No need to apologize."

Mercifully, the waitress returned with their dinner. She took the bowls away, reset the table and served their dinner. The few minutes that the whole process took wasn't enough time to erase the awkwardness that sprung up between them.

They spent the balance of their meal murmuring about how good the food was and how perfect the weather.

Layla hadn't felt so uncertain in a long time. One minute Maurice was charming and sexy. The next minute he was an impenetrable brick wall. It was clear that family was off-limits. Talking about his career as a Navy SEAL was a minefield. There were doors to his life that he kept shut. To everyone or just her? She shoved a forkful of grilled salmon into her

mouth and chewed slowly while stealing a glance
at Maurice.

As rigid as he sat, as stern as his expression was
set, intermittently she would catch flashes, just a
glimmer of vulnerability and a hurt that wasn't connected to his injury. It was reflected in his eyes or
the softening of his mouth.

Maurice Lawson was a gorgeous, sexy, complex
being of contradictions. She wanted to get to know
him better, peel away the armor that he shielded himself with, but she didn't believe that he would let her.
Besides, after tonight's fiasco she probably wouldn't
get the chance.

Chapter 8

It had been a week since he'd had dinner with Layla. A week since he'd felt the healing of her touch, the pleasure of her presence. He knew he'd made a mess of things during dinner and she probably thought… well he didn't know what she thought but it couldn't be good.

He took his cup of tea and slowly made his way out to the covered porch. Another glorious day— alone.

How could she know about the unbridgeable rift between him and his family, the reasons why he'd cut himself off from them? She couldn't. No one did. Except his uncle Branford. The almighty and powerful Senator Branford Lawson. He knew what he'd done and for that Maurice would never forgive him and by extension his family.

He leaned against the post and set his cane against it. He sipped his tea. For more than a decade the hurt had festered and bloomed into a living, breathing thing. He'd entered the military to get away and to find a means to expel the emotional pain by enduring the physical, by putting himself in danger, by taking unimaginable risks. It helped—until that night in the mountains.

Absently he massaged his injured thigh, the constant memory to his own failures. He closed his eyes and inhaled deeply, remembering the heat of Layla's touch, the magic of her fingers and the relief she brought not only to his body but to his wounded soul. She came to him in his dreams, chasing the nightmares away. She would reach for him and he would stretch out his hand and when he was only inches away from her fingertips he would wake up to the searing, throbbing pain.

He looked out toward the main building and stilled. Layla was walking along the path, carrying a backpack. She was heading in his direction.

Moments later she stood in front of him, looking up into his face from the step below the porch.

"Hi." She offered a hesitant smile.

"Hi."

Layla shifted her backpack from her right shoulder to her left. "How are you?"

"Okay, and you?"

"Busy."

"How'd you manage to get away? I'd think you would be pretty busy around this time."

"I decided to make a house call today."

He frowned slightly. "House call?"

"To you. I asked at the front desk which one was your cottage." She lifted her chin almost daring him to say something to send her away.

"Why?" His jaw tightened.

Layla placed her foot on the step. "I learned long ago in my training that it takes more than one session to make a real difference. So, I figured I'd have to come to the mountain."

His studied her for a moment. His mouth softened. "Really?"

A flicker of a smile lit her eyes. "Yes, really. I can prove it—if you let me."

Maurice angled his head to the side. "How do you plan to do that?"

She dropped her backpack at her feet and opened it, displaying the contents. "I have everything I need. The only thing missing is a willing candidate for my extensive skills."

Maurice tossed his head back and laughed, a deep, soulful sound that wrapped around her with its joyful noise. "Well, Ms. Brooks," he said, slowly sobering, "since you've come this long way, I'd be less than a gentleman if I denied you."

She bent and closed her bag, lifted it onto her shoulder and stepped up on the porch landing. "My sentiments exactly."

As much as he didn't want to, Maurice reached for his cane, but he wanted to be with Layla more. He led the way inside.

Layla released a breath of relief as she followed Maurice inside. When she'd made up her mind that she was going to put her doubts and insecurities on the back burner all she could do was hope that when she wound up on Maurice's front door it would be at the moment when there was the slightest chink in his armor and she could slip in. She smiled inside. He may be a Navy SEAL but she had some stealth moves of her own.

"Can I get you anything?" Maurice asked once they were inside.

"No, thanks. You can tell me where I can set up."

Maurice looked around. A moment of adorable bewilderment etched itself on his face. He ran his hand across his chin.

"Not many choices. I don't think the couch will work. Legs too long." His gaze bounced around the room and finally landed on Layla.

"If you don't mind we can set up in your bedroom," she suggested, trying for professional and not seductive.

His right brow flickered just a hair. He gave a slight shrug. "All right. The bedroom is this way."

His cottage was similar to hers in design except that because of her cottage's location on the path, her rooms were on the opposite side.

Maurice pushed open the bedroom door. The striped blue-and-white sheets were twisted on the bed as if someone had been in a life-and-death struggle with them.

"I wasn't expecting company," he said making his way to the bed to straighten the sheets.

"I can do that," she offered, dropped her bag with a thud on the floor and walked to the bed. "I have a sheet that I use to keep the oils from getting on the bed." She stripped the sheets from the bed and placed them in a pile on the floor.

Maurice watched, amused and a bit put off by her take-charge attitude. He was the one accustomed to giving orders and having them followed not the other way around. He wasn't sure how he felt about it.

Once she'd stripped the bed she pulled out her sheets from her bag. The top was soft cotton with a light lining on the opposite side. She spread it out on the bed and tucked the edges under the mattress. She returned to her bag and began laying out the items that she would need: her oils, the burners, a towel and a smock to put over her clothes and a portable headrest.

"I'm going to close the blinds and pull the curtains, okay?"

Maurice was leaning against the dresser with his

arms folded tightly across his chest marveling at how swiftly she had insinuated herself into his space. Within moments the room was bathed in dimness as if the sun had suddenly set.

Layla set up an oil burner on the nightstands on either side of the king-sized bed and lit them. She pulled a CD player out of her bag and put the music on. The room was slowly awash in soft light, heady scents and the soothing sounds of waterfalls and nature.

Maurice felt the tension ease from his shoulders and the tightness in his gut.

Layla slipped on her smock, tied the strings in front of her and was thankful that the light hid her shaking hands and the music drowned out the drumbeat of her heart. What made her think that this was a brilliant idea in the first place? The bravado that she felt when she hatched this little scheme was somewhere on the other side of that bedroom door—where she should have stayed and been safe.

"Ummm, you can change," Layla said, and was mortified that her voice sounded like a ten-year-old girl. "Or not." She swallowed, loving the way his sweatpants hung just right from his hips

Maurice gazed down at his not dressed for company attire. He pulled his T-shirt over his head and dropped it on top of the dresser.

Layla stifled a gasp when she set eyes on the expanse of his chest. Her pulse beat picked up a notch while heat pooled in her center. Was he going to step out of his pants—right here, right in front of her?

"Excuse me. I'll be right back." He went into the adjoining bathroom and shut the door behind him.

Layla took a shaky breath and all but crumpled on the bed. This was not a good idea. She paced in a nervous circle and then the door swung open and she froze in place.

Maurice had a towel wrapped around his sculpted middle. He was a glorious sight to behold. He eased over to the bed and sat down on the side.

"Ready when you are," he said, looking up at her, taking in her silky cinnamon brown skin, the wide luminous brown eyes and the way that one tendril of hair always slipped out from behind her ear.

Layla licked her dried lips. "You can, um, stretch out, get comfortable, with your head at the foot of the bed. Place it in the headrest." She quickly turned away and reached for her bottle of oil. She drew in a breath of the aromatic scent of the burning oil that was mixed with the natural maleness of Maurice. The bottle slipped from her fingers and tumbled to the floor. They both reached for it together and came within a heartbeat away from each other's lips.

Their gazes connected in the twilight and Layla could feel the warmth of his breath brush erotically against her face. Her hand encircled the bottle and slowly she stood. Her chest rose and fell in rapid succession. She swallowed. "Let's…get started," she whispered.

Maurice slid up on the bed and slowly turned over onto his stomach. He stretched his arms down at his sides.

Layla briskly rubbed her hands together to warm them then squirted a quarter size dot of oil into her palm. She moved the oil between her hands until they were coated and slick and then slowly placed her hands on his broad shoulders.

An inexplicable burst of energy rose up her arms. Her eyes fluttered closed as she allowed the sensation to envelop her. It was she who was here to bring relief, use her skills to ease his pain, yet touching him, set off something inside of her that she'd never before experienced. This was why she'd sought him out, to regain the feeling of being alive again after being dead inside for so long.

As she pressed her fingers into the muscles of his shoulders and his back, ran her hands along the tendons and muscles, her body came alive as if ignited from the inside.

She moved down to the small of his back then to his thighs. Expertly she reapplied the oil without completely removing her hands from his skin. Her fingers brushed over the thick, deep scar on his thigh. He flinched and she could feel him withdraw, slip away. She refocused, zeroing in on that part of him that he believed imperfect, his badge of weakness, and channeled the healing energy of her touch as she moved in gentle stroke, heightening and then lessening the pressure, willing the pain away.

By degrees she felt his body relax and give in to the sensation. Her own body was so hot as she worked his over, not from exertion but pure sensual stimulation. Her hardened nipples ached against her clothing and the dampness between her legs begged for attention. Inadvertently, a moaned escaped her lips.

Her eyes flew open. *No.*

Maurice lifted his head, turned in her direction and their hot gazes combusted. His arm came up from his side and his hand clasped her wrist.

Layla inhaled a sharp breath and her eyes widened. Maurice's grip tightened. He managed to turn half onto his side and pulled her down onto the bed next to him.

Her chest heaved. He reached up and cupped the back of her head in his hand and pulled her toward him.

"If you don't want this…tell me now."

A rush of want welled up inside of her, and she knew in the instant that she lowered her head to meet his moist lips that Maurice would be the only one to extinguish the fire that had flooded her veins.

Lights exploded behind her closed lids when her lips met his. Something deep within her began to bloom and uncurl as she sank against him and his hard, roped arms snaked around her and pulled her closer. His mouth was so sweet, like a tropical fruit and the feel of his tongue dancing with hers made her spine literally tingle.

The fit, the taste, the touch was perfect. The hum of electricity vibrated in the room like a third person.

Maurice groaned against her mouth. His fingers splayed across her back, kneading her spine until she was like putty in his hands.

Layla's breath hitched when she felt the bulge of his erection press against her stomach. Instinctively, she adjusted her length on the bed so that she could capture the epicenter of his maleness in the hot crevice between her tight thighs.

They melded together as if an artist had carved them as one entity.

Maurice ran his hands through the length of her hair, down the curve of her back to the rise of her behind that he cupped and pulled toward him so that she was flush against the pulse of his desire.

Layla moaned as her body ignited with the realization that he wanted her as badly as she wanted him. Her thoughts spun. What was she doing? She didn't know this man, yet everything about him felt as if she did. In some deep part of her she knew him. It didn't make sense, but neither did what she was doing.

She caressed his bare back, and then threaded her fingers through the soft natural curl of his hair. Maurice pulled his mouth from hers only to trail hot, wet kisses along the cord of her neck, across her collarbone to the tiny pulse that beat out of time at the base of her throat. Her whole body shuddered. He held her closer and his groan of desire enflamed her own.

Somehow he managed to slide his hand between their bodies and he pulled the loosely knotted tie of her smock belt and in a single swift motion his hands were under her T-shirt and on her heated skin. Her tummy quivered beneath his touch. By torturous degrees his hands made a slow path upward, until the tips of his fingers brushed against the underside of her bra.

Maurice tipped his head back far enough to be able to look into her eyes. "Take it off."

The ragged longing in his voice resonated all the way down to her center. And although she was never good at taking orders, she was willing to make an exception this time.

She sat up on her knees, removed her smock and then pulled her T-shirt over her head. Her heart raced a mile a minute and she was sure he could hear it.

"Don't stop," he urged with that chocolate and cinnamon gaze of his boring into her.

Layla reached behind her and unsnapped her bra. She let her arms fall to her sides.

Maurice's eyes traversed her body from head to toe. The barest hint of a smile twitched his lips. He drew in a long breath. He reached up and slid one strap off of her right shoulder. Layla held her breath.

He did the same with the other side. The full rise of her very aroused breasts held her bra in place and somewhere in the back of her head she was thrilled and relieved that she'd picked the "good" undies today.

Maurice pushed himself up into a half-sitting position and with a strength that startled her, lifted her from her spot to straddle his waist and settle right on the hard rise that pressed against and taunted her.

"I want to look at you," he said in a raw whisper. "I hope you don't mind." He peeled the right cup from her breast to expose one and then the other. He cupped them in his hands the best he could, gently squeezing, their fullness overflowing his palms. His thumbs and forefingers teased her nipples, softly tugging and elongating them and she nearly pooled into a heap on top of him.

"Stand up," he said, the simple command sounding more like an erotic caress.

Layla was pretty sure her wobbly legs would give out on her but she did as he asked, wondering what he had in mind.

She stood above him on the bed, her legs splayed on either side of his body. She looked down into his face. He didn't take his eyes off of her as he pulled the towel away from around his waist and tossed it to the floor. Layla gasped when she glimpsed him, sure that the dim lighting was playing tricks on her.

She couldn't take all of him inside her. She simply couldn't.

"Take off the rest," he said while he stroked her legs, making her unsteadiness far worst.

Her mind was in chaos, shifting between unimaginable want and reasonableness then back again. It had been more than a year since she'd been with a man, experiencing what it was like to be wanted and giving into that want. Her raging hormones played havoc with her body. Unimaginable want won.

She undid the button of her shorts and then slid the zipper down. The room was engulfed in heat or maybe it was her. All she knew for certain was that she was on fire and it was getting harder to breathe. Every inch of her wanted release. She shimmied her shorts across her hips and down her legs and stepped out of them. She tossed them onto the floor. His gaze scorched her inner thighs.

Maurice ran his hands along the inside of her thighs and they began to tremble as if tiny electrodes were under her skin. His fingers roamed upward until he reached the apex of her thighs, protected only by pale blue satin and lace. He cupped her sex in his palm, pressed his thumb against her clitoris and teased until she exploded into a million tiny pieces. Her startled cry was hoarse and ragged. She felt her legs give out and her body falling forward as the climax ripped through her.

Maurice used his other hand to brace her body,

holding her up with his hand pressed firmly against her belly, forcing her to experience the tumultuous orgasm standing up above him. Slowly he eased her down and before she could catch her breath, he'd turned her onto her back. He didn't wait for her to take her panties off. He did it for her. His hands went to her heat, finding her wet and throbbing. She moaned and he slid a finger inside. Her hips spontaneously arched in response. He moved his finger around in slow, maddening circles and then even slower in and out before inserting finger number two.

Her insides clenched around them. Her belly quivered as her hips rose and fell to meet each stroke of his expert hands. Her sighs had turned to whimpers as she felt the build up again. *So soon*—she managed to think. Not again, she wasn't ready, she couldn't be. But her mind was no longer in charge, her body was.

Maurice placed tiny, incendiary kisses behind her ear, across her neck, along her throat down to the rise of her breast. He took one nipple into his mouth and her body rose up off the bed. All the air was lodged in her throat as his tongue moved in tantalizing circles around the hardened bud and the tips of his teeth nibbled ever so seductively.

She was one live wire now, unable to distinguish one amazing sensation from the other.

"I'll ask you again," he said lifting his mouth from the succulent taste of her breast.

Layla's eyes fluttered open. Everything was out of focus.

"Are you sure you want this?"

"Yes," she managed.

He stretched across her and dug in the nightstand drawer. He pulled out a condom. He stared into her eyes, tore the pack open with his teeth. He pulled the soft, nearly translucent rubber out of its protective pack, and braced on his knees, he slowly rolled it along his considerable length.

Layla watched in utter fascination. She'd never thought that watching a man put on a condom could be such a turn-on.

A dark, almost dangerous look hung in his eyes. He pushed her legs apart and bent them at the knee. He kissed the inside of her thighs. She drew in a sharp breath. And then he was inside of her.

She cried out as the sensation of being filled and stretched settled around her. Maurice, remained perfectly still as her body adjusted and then he began to push further inside of her, slow and easy.

Instinct took over and her hips rose and fell to meet his slow and deliberate thrusts. They found their rhythm and moved in harmony, the sensations building with intensity. Heat suffused them. The sounds of their pleasure filled the room—Layla's soft cries and Maurice's guttural groans combined for their own unique sound.

The tempo began to quicken. Layla felt her release

building from the soles of her feet, scurrying up her legs, between her thighs. Her scalp tingled. Her hips arched and banged against his downward thrust. He captured a needy nipple in his mouth, sucked, and her entire world exploded.

Maurice was locked in the vortex of her climax. He rode her faster, harder. She screamed. His entire body stiffened and then he erupted inside of her.

Chapter 9

When Layla opened her eyes, she was alone. For a moment she couldn't figure out where she was. Her body ached. She was sticky between her legs and she was naked.

She sat up and looked around and reality hit her. *Maurice's room.* She covered her face with her hands and groaned in mortification. What the hell had she done?

Quickly she scrambled out of bed and began looking around for her clothes, picking them up piece by piece and putting them on while silently praying that he didn't walk through the door. He was probably off somewhere thinking what an easy lay she was. Oh, God. She had to get out of there.

She fastened her shorts. Her head snapped around the room. She peered under the sheets and the bed. She couldn't find her bra. *Damn it*. She tugged on her T-shirt, grabbed her smock and tied it tightly around her waist. Her tender nipples brushed against the fabric. She drew in air from between her teeth when her clit throbbed in response.

The flame beneath the oil burners had gone out. She snatched them off the nightstand, and dumped them into her knapsack along with the massage oils and towels.

Layla took one last look around, ran her hand through her hair and groaned again. She must look like a hot mess or rather a horny woman that just experienced the greatest sex in her adult life. A tremor of memory scurried up her spine.

She nearly sprinted to the bedroom door and pulled it open. No sign of Maurice. With as much dignity as she had left, she crossed the open living space to the front door and stepped outside. The warm, salty air assuaged her senses.

"Leaving?"

Her heart stopped. She snapped her head to the left. Maurice was sitting on the cushioned bench, near the corner of the porch, partially hidden beneath the overhang and the dimming sunlight, sipping something from a tall, iced glass.

She swallowed. "Yeah, I'd better get going." She

tried to find a place to look and adjusted her knapsack onto her shoulder.

Slowly he stood up and she was once again transfixed by his eyes and the way his sleek dark brows swept across them. And then he was standing right in front of her, close enough that she had to lift her chin to look up at him. She could feel heat radiate off of his body. She clutched her bag of goods.

Maurice's finger lifted and trailed a soft line from her ear down across her jaw. She wanted to back away but she couldn't move. Her insides curled deliciously in response. A glimmer of something close to a smile played with his mouth.

"Thank you...*for coming*...I feel much better."

She swallowed over the enormous knot of emotion that wedged in her throat. *What was he saying? What did he really mean?* "Good. I'm glad," she eked out. She took a step back as much to make her getaway as to keep distance between her and his raw magnetism.

Quickly she turned and hurried along the pathway to safety. She thought she heard him call out to her but she didn't dare look back. It was probably her imagination anyway. And then for some inexplicable reason tears welled in her eyes, clouding her vision. She tugged on her bottom lip to stifle a sob. What had she done?

She ducked her head as she hurried past a couple strolling in the opposite direction. She was positive that anyone setting eyes on her would know that she had just given up the goods to a man that she barely knew. A sudden visual of her body practically suspended above him in the throes of a wicked orgasm flamed in front of her. A whimper slipped out. She shook her head briskly and ran up the one step leading to her front door. She twisted the knob and practically fell inside.

Tears that she'd held in check rolled down her cheeks. She wrapped her arms protectively around her body allowing the closed door to support her weight before she slid down to the floor, dropped her head to her knees and wept.

After a long, hot shower, Layla moved around her cottage dazed and edgy. How was she going to be able to stay at The Port after what had happened? She poured some chilled white wine into a glass and then sat down at the breakfast bar. She stared out of the wide bay window at the last rays of the blazing sun as it slipped below the horizon, casting beacons of orange and gold across the slightly rippling water.

She couldn't face him. And heaven only knew what he must think of her. She cringed and took a swallow of wine. There had to be a way out of this mess that she'd found herself in. Desiree had gone all out to get the spa up and running specifically for her. She couldn't in good conscience leave her high and dry and go back to the city.

She sighed heavily and took another sip of wine. Her gaze drifted off from the beauty beyond and landed someplace earlier in the day when reason had no place in her head. She'd been caressed, and touched, kissed and sexed and turned on in ways that she didn't know were possible. A wanton smile pulled at the corner of her mouth.

It was damn good. "Humph, humph, humph." She knew it had been a long time, and she may have forgotten just how good great sex could feel, but this was off the charts. Maurice Lawson knew what to do with and to a woman. And Layla had the deep suspicion that what he showed her today was only the appetizer before the main course. Goose bumps galloped along her arms and down her back.

She shook her head hoping to shake free from the thoughts and images of Maurice Lawson—to no avail. She took another sip of wine and a long deep breath and her insides jumped. She could smell him, his scent that triggered something deep and carnal inside of her. His scent had seeped into her pores and all the body wash and scrubbing hadn't gotten rid of it.

Her vibrating cell phone shimmied across the counter. She snatched it up and looked at the lighted face. *Desiree.* Briefly she shut her eyes. What was she going to tell her friend?

She slid her finger across the screen to unlock the phone and pressed the telephone icon. "Hey," she greeted, pushing cheer into her voice.

"Hey, yourself. I stopped by the spa to check on

you but it was locked up tight. Everything okay? Please don't tell me business is dwindling already," she said with laughter in her voice.

"No, not at all. I cleared my schedule for this afternoon." She paused. "I needed to take care of a few things that's all."

Desiree was silent for a moment. "Are you sure you're okay, because you sound funny? Whatsup?"

Layla blew out a breath. Over the years she and Desiree had shared some of their most intimate secrets, dreams and desires. They'd been there for each other through break-ups and make-ups and everything in between.

She took a sip of her wine and set the glass down. "I just had the greatest sex of my life with one of your guests," she blurted out in one long string of words.

"OMG. I'm coming over right now. Do. Not. Move. And I'm bringing wine!" She disconnected the call before Layla had a chance to react.

Layla lifted the glass to her mouth and finished off her drink. "Here we go," she muttered.

Desiree sat with her legs tucked beneath her on Layla's overstuffed sofa that was a rich buttercream in a simple jacquard fabric of seascapes. The sheer floor-to-ceiling drapes in the same airy color were seductively caressed by the light breeze that blew in from the open window and the French doors. The entire space begged relaxation, from the cool woods of the floors, and the sea breeze to the sensuous furnishings, but none of that settled the jangling inside Layla's stomach. Not even her fourth glass of wine.

"I am still in shock," Desiree said, eyeing her friend over the rim of her wineglass.

"You! How do you think I feel?"

Desiree snorted her laughter. "From what you told me—*damned good!* I think that was the term you used." She slapped her thigh in merriment.

Layla pursed her lips in annoyance. "Very funny. This is serious, Desi. How can I look him in the face after this?"

Desiree arched a brow in thought, sipped her wine. "Hmm. Look, you are both adults. Handle it like an adult. Maybe he's feeling just as awkward as you are. Your crazy behind was bold enough to go over there in the first place, so be bold when you see him again."

Layla sputtered her drink. "What!"

"I don't mean that kind of bold. I mean talk to him. Be honest. You're obviously attracted to him." She shrugged. "See where it goes. If nothing comes of it at least you got the cootie cobwebs cleared," she snickered.

Layla's eyes and mouth opened wide. "You are so awful!" She shook her head. "I swear...can't tell you anything."

"I know. I'm sorry. I'm just messing with you. It's just so good to hear you have that raw rasp in your voice when you to talk about a man. I mean, come on, sis, it's been over a year. You're a grown, healthy, beautiful, intelligent woman. You deserve to get your groove on, too." She lowered her voice and took Layla's hand. "Brent left some real scars, I know that. He got your emotions all twisted and stomped all over them. He made you lose trust in men and relationships. But every man isn't Brent. Maurice Lawson may be or may not be the one for you, but it's time to move on with your life anyway."

Layla heaved a sigh. "He has issues."

Desiree cocked her head to the side and gave her that *are you serious look*. "And you don't?"

"Fine," she huffed. "I'll take your advice."

"Good. Now let's get something to eat or I'm going to be drunk."

"But…what if we run into him?" she asked, suddenly not so sure of Desiree's plan for her new life.

"Then you smile that sweet smile of yours and ask him if he'd like to join us." Desiree unfolded herself, stood up and stretched. "Hey, I just remembered. Melanie called me earlier. She's back and definitely wants to get together. Just us girls."

"Sounds good to me."

"And…as you know, Melanie has her own connections to the Lawson family. Maybe she can give you some details on Maurice. She's practically family. Her husband, Claude, is chief of staff for Maurice's uncle Branford."

"Get out." Layla blinked back her surprise, stood and followed Desiree to the door.

"As a matter of fact, let me give her a call. Maybe she's up for a visit."

Chapter 10

Melanie squealed in delight and wrapped Layla in a tight embrace from the instant she flung her door open. "Oh, it is so good to see you. It's been way too long." She draped her arm around Layla's shoulder and ushered her inside.

"So what am I, an old shoe," Desiree whined, feigning offense. She shut the door and huffed in behind them.

"Let's sit out back. I made a pitcher of mimosas," Melanie said, beaming and hugging Layla close.

"You look fabulous," Layla said. They entered the enclosed veranda that looked out onto the pool. "Marriage totally agrees with you."

Melanie's luminous brown eyes sparkled. "That's

what love will do for you," she said, her voice filled with girlish delight. "Never thought I'd find it again after losing Steven all those years ago. So I threw myself into the family business—finding perfect matches for the perfect people. The Platinum Society became my world." She laughed. "Who knew! Come. Sit. Relax."

Always the consummate hostess, Melanie took the carafe of mimosas and poured some into the three goblets, then took a seat on the lounge chair. She raised her glass. "To good friends…"

"Friendship," they chorused.

"So tell me," Melanie began, "what's been going on, girl? How is life in New York?"

Layla took a soothing sip of her cool drink. "Hmmm. This is good." She set her glass down on the table. "Hey, what can I say? Things went from fabulous to WTH." She tucked one leg beneath her. "Lost my job at the paper, unemployment started running out, wound up taking a job at a lounge in the West Village, lost my man. But I did get to test the waters of doing my own thing with massages. And I love it." She gave a half smile. "Fortunately, I learned good financial lessons from your mother Aunt Carolyn. Otherwise…" She shook her head and her voice drifted off.

Melanie blew out a breath. "Well, you're here now." She reached over and patted Layla's thigh. "And in a few weeks we are going to be partying!"

She snorted a laugh. "Humph, we can start now," she teased.

"Speaking of partying, you will never guess who is staying at The Port," Desiree said.

Layla flashed her a warning look, which Desiree ignored.

"Who?"

"Maurice Lawson."

Melanie frowned. "Maurice Lawson." She ran the name across her tongue then angled her head to the side and looked at Desiree. "Branford's nephew?" Her right brow arched.

Desiree slowly bobbed her head.

"Wow," Melanie said in wonder. Her mind trailed off to a long ago conversation of the mysterious Maurice Lawson. "No one in his family has seen him in almost ten years. At least that's what I recall Claude telling me. I knew Branford had a brother, David, but I'd never met David's son. Apparently something major happened after David died and Maurice totally cut himself off from the family." She stirred herself back from her reverie and gazed at her friends. "And he's here." She shook her head in amazement. "Go figure. I wonder if his family knows. I swear I thought Claude told me he was in the military or something."

"Navy SEAL," Layla offered. "Tall, built, handsome, sexy, dripping in warm chocolate..."

Melanie gave her an arched look. "Hmmm. Impressive."

"And she slept with him," Desiree added like a kid itching to tell a secret.

Layla's mouth dropped open. She thought they were going to find out about Maurice and *she* would be the one to ease out the information about her afternoon sexcapade. She tossed Desiree a scathing look and rolled her eyes so hard she thought they would stick in the back of her head.

Desiree lowered her head and snickered behind her glass.

"Well…dayum, girl," Melanie laughed. "Good for you. But should I make that a statement or a question?"

"I barely know the man," she blurted. "I went over there *only* with the intention of giving him a massage," she said, emphasizing the word *only*. "And one thing just led to the other and the next thing I knew…"

"'I had the time of my life…'" Desiree sang off-key from the *Dirty Dancin'* theme song. She slapped her thighs and cracked up laughing.

Layla wagged a finger at Desiree while looking at Melanie who was fighting back her own laughter. "*Her* I'm going to kill. I swear." She reached for her glass to hide her smirk.

"So…" Melanie breathed. "What happened after…"

"I pretty much ran back to my cottage."

Melanie frowned. "Why, for heaven sake?"

"I don't know. I was...embarrassed. I felt like a call girl."

Melanie pursed her lips in annoyance then she leaned toward Layla. "Listen. You are a grown woman. He didn't pick you up on some corner. Did he leave money on the nightstand?"

Layla shook her head.

"So what makes you think he believes anything less of you?"

Layla tugged on her bottom lip with her teeth. "We had dinner the week before," she added meekly. "He'd come to the spa earlier for a massage...and," she hesitated, trying to find the words, "there was this *thing* that happened between us. I don't even know how to explain it."

"Humph," Melanie hummed in appreciation. "I know just what you mean. And when it defies explanation giiirrrlll," she held up her palm as if testifying, "you have something on your hands."

They all broke into laughter and gave high fives.

"Whew..." Desiree exclaimed, and wiped the corners of her eyes.

"Okay, so now that ya'll are all in my business, what do I do? He must think I'm..."

"That's just it, you don't know what he thinks because you ran out of there like someone was chasing you," Melanie scolded. "Look, what happened, happened. Put your big girl panties on. The next move is up to him. Either he will make it or he won't. Whichever way things turn out, you have nothing to lose and may have plenty to gain. And you got yourself an afternoon you won't forget for a long time in the process."

"You got that right," Desiree piped in.

Layla finished off her mimosa and poured herself another one. "Okay." She bobbed her head.

"I'm going to do some checking. As a matter of fact—" She stretched toward her cell phone that was on the circular glass and chrome table. Quickly she scrolled through her contacts and hit the name she was looking for.

Layla and Desiree gave each other puzzled looks.

Melanie tapped her nail on the arm of the chair while the phone rang. "Hello, Rafe, it's Melanie." She winked at her two friends. "Hey, sweetie, still breaking hearts everywhere…of course I'm still with my husband…" She tossed her head back and laughed. "Oh you are so awful…behave. Listen, you'll never guess who's here at the Harbor…"

The next morning Layla unlocked the door to the spa and stepped inside. The cool, dim confines were exactly what she needed. She hesitated to take off her shades, fearful of what the light would do to her eyes and her mildly pounding head.

She'd definitely had too much to drink the night before. That was so unlike her. But, the truth was everything that she'd done since she got the invite from Melanie and then accepted Desiree's crazy offer had been unlike her: from putting her fledgling business on hiatus, having wild uninhibited sex with a man she barely knew, to drinking mimosas with the girls all night.

Lincoln drove the two miles from The Port to Melanie's estate on the Harbor to pick up his wife, who giggled all the way to the car while Layla opted to spend the night at Melanie's lavish abode.

Melanie had dropped Layla off at her cottage on her way into Manhattan for a meeting with some potential clients. She'd showered, dressed and stopped off at the restaurant for a quick breakfast, praying as she sipped her coffee that she wouldn't run into Maurice. She wasn't ready to face him yet, especially with her thoughts still fuzzy.

She dropped her oversized tote bag in the chair and booted up the computer to check for her appointments. Her first appointment was at 10:30. She had a half hour to prepare.

While she checked the sauna, showers and massage rooms, she thought about what Rafe had conveyed to Melanie about Maurice. Basically, he'd been MIA from the family for almost a decade. Following his father David's death—an apparent suicide—Maurice took off, cut all ties with the family and joined the Navy. It seemed that no one knew exactly what happened between Maurice and Branford before Maurice took off, but they'd had a major blow up argument at the family home in Louisiana. Maurice stormed out, accusing Branford for his father's death. When Branford's children tried to ask him about it, Branford refused to discuss it.

Rafe had said that he knew his father had been devastated by what happened between him and Maurice but he would never talk about it. Rafe did say that he got a postcard from him about five years earlier, which was the first time anyone had heard from Maurice, and that was how they knew he was in the Navy. Rafe was surprised that Maurice was stateside. He'd written on his card that he had plans to never come back.

Layla took fresh towels from the bin and rolled them before she stacked them on the shelves. Why would Maurice believe that his uncle was responsible for his father's death? Did anyone else believe the same thing? One thing she did know for certain, when you were as politically powerful and connected as the Lawsons, you could make bad news disappear.

She shook her head to dispel the ugly thoughts. She knew nothing about what happened ten years ago, other than it broke up a family and sent a man thousands of miles away, only to return not only emotionally scarred but physically scarred as well. She couldn't begin to imagine what Maurice had endured.

The bell over the door chimed. She glanced over

her shoulder and her insides went on high alert. Her face felt like it was on fire.

She placed the last towel in the shelf. "Hi," she was finally able to manage.

Maurice let the door close softly behind him. He stepped inside. "Morning."

She wished she could see his eyes behind his dark shades and as if in answer to her silent request he took them off and she felt herself turn to liquid when he looked at her. She leaned against the row of shelves to steady herself. "You're out early."

"I believe this is yours." He raised his hand and dangling from his fingers was a small brown shopping bag, the kind you get in novelty shops.

Layla's heart thumped. *Oh dayum*. She tried to look like she didn't want the floor to open and swallow her whole and had no idea if she succeeded or not. She reached for the bag and peeked inside. She shut her eyes and knew that were it not for her cinnamon brown complexion she would flame fire engine red. Her wayward bra was nestled politely inside.

She cleared her throat. "Um, thank you."

"Anytime."

Her gaze jerked to his. *What did that mean?* A shadow of a smile played around the corners of his mouth. Was he laughing at her?

She lifted her chin. "Thanks for…bringing this." She glanced around the room. "I uh, really need to get to work."

He bobbed his head. "Sure. Don't let me hold you up." He turned to leave.

"I don't usually do that kind of thing," she called out to his back.

Maurice's hand stopped on the doorknob. He looked at her over his shoulder. "Neither do I," he said softly.

Oh my. The simple declaration fluttered in her belly. She licked her lips. "How is your leg?" she asked in a small voice.

"Better. Better than it's been in a while."

Her heart felt as if it was doing somersaults in her chest. Maurice did something to her senses and the overwhelming need to touch him she was only able to contain by gripping the small shopping bag.

"Well, don't hesitate to stop by…when you need to…for a massage treatment."

"I'll keep that in mind."

"I have an opening in the schedule later this afternoon if you want to stop by," she said in a rush.

His eyes slowly stroked her up and down and she felt the heat unfurl deep inside. He released the knob and turned toward her. She stopped breathing. What choice did she have? She couldn't concentrate on breathing and succumbing to the breathtaking maleness of him at the same time.

"What time?"

She watched his lips and a flash of them suckling her nipple flashed in her head. She blinked rapidly.

He'd said something. "Um…I'm sorry. What did you ask me? My mind is in a million places at once this morning." She ran her left hand through her hair and tucked it behind her ear.

"I asked what time would work for you?" His lashes lowered ever so slightly over his eyes.

"Two o'clock."

"I'll see you then."

The best she could do was nod her head in agreement. And then he was gone and it felt like the light in the room had dimmed. A rush of air expelled from her lungs. She leaned against the desk to steady her shaky legs.

Two o'clock. He'd be back at two. Her heart sang a little song. She pressed her hands to her chest. Just a therapeutic massage. That's it. Maybe. She smiled.

Chapter 11

Layla moved through her day in a daze. It took all of her concentration to focus on her clients. She must have dropped the bottles of oil a half dozen times while she was with her customers. She lost count of how many times she had to apologize for going too deep while her mind wandered. And the hours seemed to crawl by. What would it be like with the two of them together in a dimly lit, aromatic room, with him partially clothed—after what had happened between them? She was excited and terrified at the same time.

Her last customer for the first half of her day walked out at one-thirty. Maybe this wasn't such a good idea, she thought as she busied herself with straightening up the rooms. Maybe what she should do was leave before he arrived.

She glanced up at the clock. He said two. Ten minutes. The door chimed. Her heart jumped.

"Hi." Kim closed the door behind her. "I was hoping you could squeeze me in," she said with a big smile. "I know I should have called."

"Hmmm." Layla flipped her wrist and looked at her watch. "Actually, I have a client coming in a few minutes. Can I schedule you for first thing in the morning?" She moved to the computer and pulled up the calendar.

Kim looked crestfallen. "Oh." She pouted prettily. "I could wait…"

"I'd really love to accommodate you. It's just that this afternoon is booked."

Kim blew out a breath of frustration. "Okay. Tomorrow, then. What time?" She tried to peek at the schedule.

Layla was trying to keep her fingers from trembling as she typed in Kim's information. All she wanted was for her to be gone before Maurice arrived. The vibe between the two of them was not the best the last time around, and Layla didn't want Kim to prick Maurice the wrong way.

Layla printed out the confirmation and handed it to Kim. "I'll see you tomorrow at ten-thirty. And I'll throw in a facial."

Kim's green eyes widened. "Wow. Thanks. I'll have to pop in unannounced more often."

Layla made herself laugh while her mind was saying "go, go."

"I'll see you tomorrow. Don't work too hard."

"I'll try," she responded in a singsong. She finger-waved goodbye. Her shoulders slumped and she plopped down in her chair at the sound of the door closing behind Kim.

For a moment she shut her eyes. She wasn't quite sure why she was so anxious about Kim and Maurice meeting again. It was her gut instinct that told her it would not be a good move. Whether it was or not she was glad that Kim was gone. Kim seemed a bit too astute to miss the sparks that flew between her and Maurice and she didn't want some stranger in her developing business with Mr. Navy SEAL. *If there was any business to develop.* For all she knew Maurice could simply be coming for a massage to keep his injured leg limber and pain free.

But if she had to tell the story, based on his mobility and flexibility at his cottage, his leg wasn't the problem.

The door chimed. Her body jerked. As casually as she could she looked toward the door and everything inside spun. He was simply gorgeous. Muscular but lean from years of physical training, tall, with piercing eyes, a solid jaw that she remembered trailing her fingers across, and a full rich mouth. But it was more than his physical self that drew her. There was something about Maurice Lawson that oozed sexuality and drew her like a magnet to him without him even trying. It was nothing he said, nothing in particular that he did, yet everything about him was sensual, predatory. Even his cane was sexy. He moved it in unity with his body so that it was a part of him and not a distraction but an accessory. And even more, beneath that gorgeous exterior there was a tender spot inside of him that he worked hard to keep hidden and she wanted to discover why.

She inhaled deeply to steady herself before slowly pushing up from her seat. "Hi. You made it."

A glimmer of a smile played around his mouth.

He wore a black fitted T-shirt that outlined his broad, muscular chest and a pair of faded jeans that looked cottony soft to the touch from years of wash and wear. They hung low on his waist and the image heated her blood. She ran her tongue across her lips. "Let's, uh, get you started."

Layla locked the front door then led the way to the sauna. Maurice had yet to say a word and a crazy part of her mind thought that maybe this was all her imagination and that he wasn't really there at all. But that was ridiculous. She could feel him right behind her and his delicious scent—clean, manly and all Maurice—teased her sensibilities.

"How was your morning?" she asked, his silence jangling her already frayed nerves.

She stopped in front of the sauna and turned. Her heart leapt to her throat and beat like crazy. The burning look in his eyes engulfed her, fueled the longing in the pit of her belly and sparked outward. He rested his cane against the wall. The hairs on the back of her neck tingled.

And then before she could blink, he'd slid his large hand behind the back of her head and pulled her toward him. His other arm snaked around her waist and tugged her against his erection that throbbed against her stomach.

A sharp intake of breath was all she had time for before his mouth swept down and captured hers. His warm, soft lips, grazed over hers, and his teasing tongue coaxed them open.

His kiss was sweeter than the last time. She adored the taste of him, the feel of his tongue as it played with hers, explored her mouth, possessed it.

Maurice tugged her closer, threading his fingers through her hair, molding her body to his. And then he broke the kiss and she felt as if she'd fallen from a great height. She blinked him into focus and his gaze was dark, hungry almost. She couldn't breathe.

"I've been thinking about kissing you all morning."

Her pulse was pounding so loudly in her ears that she felt her body vibrate. She took a small step back. "I've been…feeling the same way." She swallowed.

His dark eyes caressed her.

"How is your leg?" she managed to ask in a thready voice.

He glanced down at his leg and his expression shifted. The light dimmed in his eyes. "That's what I'm here for." All the warmth left his eyes.

Her heart thumped. What just happened? "Sure. Let's get you set up." She quickly turned away, not wanting Maurice to see the hurt and confusion in her eyes. She felt unbalanced. One minute he was seducing her and the next he was a complete stranger, not a man who had done things to her body that she'd only imagined were possible.

Concentrating on putting one foot in front of the other, she led the way to the sauna. She stopped, turned toward him and lifted her chin. "You know the drill." She forced herself to smile. "I'll be in the massage room when you're ready." She hurried away and shut the door behind her.

The threat of tears burned her eyes. She rested the back of her head against the closed door. What a mess. She'd made the biggest mistake a woman could make—sleeping with a man that she barely knew. This wasn't the kind of woman that she was. Ever since Brent she'd made it a point to steer clear of relationships. She wasn't like some of her friends who could have sex with a man and nothing more.

What made her think for a minute that she could handle something like this? Not to mention that it was clear that Maurice Lawson had issues of his own.

She pushed away from the door and routinely began preparing the room for her sexy, complex client. She drew in a breath of resolve. This was going to be purely professional. End of story.

Maurice lay facedown on the table. His arms were at his sides, his head facing downward through the circular cushioned opening.

The flickering lights from the candles cast soft shadows on the walls and played tricks on her eyes as she studied the muscles of his back. Her gaze traveled along his back down to the dip in his spine, the rise of his lush rear end down to the muscular thighs and toned legs. He was an exquisite specimen of a man.

Layla poured a quarter sized amount of scented oil onto her palm and then another. A part of her longed to touch him again, another part dreaded what touching him would do to her.

Maurice shifted his shoulders, nudging her out of her moment of indecision. Just do it and get it over with. Strictly business.

Pressing her lips tightly together she lowered her hands to his shoulders. A jolt of current prickled the hair on her arms. She drew a sharp breath as heat radiated through her veins. She would have sobbed had it not been that she was biting down on her lip.

Her skilled fingers instinctively did their work,

soothing, massaging, pressing into his back, down his spine, splaying out to his waist and back again.

His moan was raw. She could feel it vibrate deep beneath the smooth flesh up through to the tips of her fingers.

Without letting her hands leave his body, she moved down to his thigh. First she worked the un-injured side then skillfully moved to the other side of the table and began to work her magic on his injured leg.

Her fingers first skimmed across the raised scar then the indentation. Again, just like the first time, his body tightened, flexed as if he were about to flee. But her hands stilled him, calmed him, moved across the unwilling flesh and made it succumb.

Her hands moved in time to the slow, sensual beat of the music that she could barely hear above her thundering heart. She felt him loosening. His body hummed.

Maurice groaned and with agility that stunned her, he flipped onto his back and grabbed her wrist in a vice grip.

Her breath hitched. His eyes burned her skin. He sat up, released her wrist and swung his legs over the side. He stood. Layla's chest rose and fell in rapid succession. While she stood frozen, Maurice opened the door and walked out.

Layla blinked back her surprise. What the… Did

she hurt him? Did she do something wrong? She quickly snatched up a towel to wipe her hands and hurried out of the open door.

Chapter 12

Layla heard banging and movement coming from the changing room. She drew in a breath and stalked off in that direction.

Maurice tugged the door open. Layla gasped and came to a dead stop.

His brows were pulled together in a tight thick line. He appeared as if whatever was brewing beneath the surface could not be contained, like a volcano ready to erupt. For the first time, Layla felt a shiver of fear in his presence.

He slung his backpack over his shoulder, threw a last look at Layla that froze her veins. He started past her, letting the cane take some of his weight.

Maurice was halfway past her when Layla swung around, her good sense finally returning.

"Just wait one damned minute!"

Maurice stopped in mid-step. He glared at her over his shoulder. His brows rose as she came at him.

She crossed the short space between them and looked up into his eyes with her fists planted on her hips. "Who the hell do you think you are?" she shouted. "What am I, some insignificant," she fumbled for a word, "whatever, that you can charm, screw and dismiss at will? You're hot one minute and glacier cold the next. I may not mean anything to you and that's fine! Maybe this is something you do all the time. And that's fine, too. But the least you can be is a decent human being!" Tears threatened to tumble, but she would not give him the satisfaction of seeing her cry.

Maurice rocked his jaw slowly from side to side as if he'd been punched. "I'm not someone you want to get involved with," he said. His voice was so soft, so low, if what he said wasn't so heartbreakingly sad, it would have sounded like a love song.

Her heart clenched.

Maurice walked out.

"That is so crazy," Desiree murmured after listening intently to Layla's recounting of what had happened at the spa. She slowly forked a mouthful of salad. "And he didn't say anything else?"

Layla shook her head. The incident at the spa had shaken her in a way that was hard to explain. Maurice was a montage of conflicts that left her walking on a precipice of self doubt. She simply could not wrap her mind around him. There were moments when she saw in his eyes, felt in his touch the warmth and caring that resided inside him. But right alongside that goodness and light was unreachable darkness, an anguish that hovered just beneath the surface. What had happened to him? That was the question that taunted her, dared her to find out.

"Listen, it seems that Maurice Lawson's baggage is even too heavy for him to carry. Let it go, La." She reached across the table and covered Layla's hand with her own. "It simply wasn't meant to be more than what it was. A hot, crazy one night affair."

Layla sighed heavily. "Yeah. I guess." Her gaze drifted off. As much as she wanted to dismiss it all and move on, she knew that there was a connection. She knew that he felt it too. She looked across the table at her friend. "What if Lincoln had let you go? What if he'd decided that all your baggage was too heavy, Desi?" she asked, really needing an answer.

Desiree lowered her eyes. Her mouth tightened for a moment. "That was different. We had a relationship."

"One that you walked out on."

"This isn't about me." She paused a beat. "Layla, you barely know this guy. Actually you don't know him at all."

Layla picked up her water glass and took a long

swallow. Slowly she set the glass down. "You're right," she said on a breath.

"I know me and Melanie told you to go for it. We were wrong. I'm sorry. Don't make yourself crazy over this."

Layla angled her head to the side. "It's not your fault. I'm a big girl. I knew what I was doing."

"Still…"

"I don't want to talk about Maurice Lawson anymore. He is a closed chapter in my book of life."

"That's more like it." Desiree raised her glass of iced tea. "To moving on."

Layla touched her glass to Desiree's. "To moving on."

"Speak of the devil," Desiree said, barely moving her lips. Layla started to turn. "Don't look. He's coming this way," she said from between her teeth.

Layla's stomach fluttered.

And then he was standing right beside her. She could feel his heat. She inhaled his scent. Her pulse raced.

"Hello, Layla…Mrs. Armstrong."

"Hello. I hope you're enjoying your stay."

"I am. Thanks."

Layla dared to look up and she went tumbling into the depths of his eyes and was lost.

"Sorry to interrupt. I stopped by the spa…but it was locked up. I wanted to make an appointment."

She blinked back her surprise. "Oh. I closed early today."

"What time do you open tomorrow? I'll stop by then."

"At ten, but I have a full schedule tomorrow."

Desiree watched the unmistakable electricity snap back and forth between them and needed to duck out of the way or get struck. "I should get back to my office. Take my seat," she said in an almost breathy whisper that took Layla by surprise.

Layla's gaze darted to Desiree who was already rising from her seat as if under some sort of spell. Layla fully understood that magic.

"Layla, I'll see you tomorrow. We have shopping to do."

"Okay," she said.

Maurice eased into Desiree's vacated seat. He rested his cane against his thigh and placed his hands on top of the table.

Layla rested against the back of the chair and pressed her knees together to keep her legs from trembling. She linked her fingers together.

Maurice's dark eyes glided lazily across her face, down her throat to the V-opening in her blouse.

Her skin grew warmer. Butterflies fluttered low in her belly.

"I owe you an apology," he finally said, the words moved across her in a tender caress.

Her breathing escalated. She tore her eyes away from him to gain some balance. "For what?"

"For not being a decent human being."

The muscles in her chest tightened making it hard to breathe.

"I was hoping to make it up to you."

"You don't have to make anything up to me."

"Have dinner with me."

Her gaze jumped to his face and the intensity in his eyes was her undoing.

"Why should I?"

"So that I can prove to you that I can be a decent human being."

She started to reach for her glass of water but her hands were shaking. She kept them knotted on the table instead.

"Tomorrow?" He tipped his head to the side and looked at her from beneath those long, lush lashes. "Mojitos on me."

This coaxed a small smile from her. She pushed out a tiny breath. "Fine. Tomorrow."

"Seven?"

She bobbed her head in agreement.

A slow smile moved across his mouth and lit the hidden fire behind his eyes.

Damn he was gorgeous and *dangerous*.

Maurice reached for his cane and slowly stood. He glanced down at her. "Looking forward to seeing you tomorrow."

He strolled out, his limp barely noticeable, more a swagger than a limp. Layla was finally able to breathe only to realize how damp she was between her legs.

Layla and Desiree spent the latter part of the next afternoon in town shopping for an outfit for Desiree and Lincoln's anniversary party.

"Do you think I should ask Maurice to come to the party at Melanie's?"

Desiree held up a Vera Wang short cocktail dress in a stunning combination of platinum and black. Desiree looked at Layla above the dress that she held against her body.

"Do you want to?"

"I'm not sure."

"Maybe you should see how tonight goes and what he has to say for himself before you ask."

"True." She picked up a sleeveless teal dress with a heart-shaped neckline that gathered in front and fell to just above her knees.

"That's you," Desiree said emphatically.

"And if I don't take this dress, you will," Layla returned.

Desiree giggled. "What are you going to wear tonight? You know it has to be a knockout."

"Hmm, good question. Guess I still need to shop!"

They linked arms with their choices in tow and continued looking.

It was ten minutes to seven and Layla was as nervous as if she'd never been out on a dinner date in her life. She'd checked her makeup and adjusted her dress more times than she could count. Every time she heard a noise her heart leapt to her throat.

She paced her bedroom and then the living room and kitchen like a woman possessed. At precisely seven, there was a knock on her front door. She froze. Suddenly her mind went blank. The knock came again, jerking her alert. She swallowed, ran her hands nervously down her dress and then walked to the door.

She pulled it open and stopped breathing at the sight of him.

He was clad in black from head to toe. The brushed cotton shirt was open three buttons down and tucked into the waistband of sleek black slacks that fit him to perfection. And his scent. Oh, his scent. It went straight to her head.

"You look beautiful," he said almost reverently. His gaze drank her in, the way her sleek brows swept over dark, almond shaped eyes and that mouth that he remembered so well. Her dress gently teased her curves and floated right above her knees to reveal her long, shapely legs.

"Thank you," she managed.

"The midnight blue does something to your skin."

The words slid along her bare arms and teased her breasts that had risen to attention.

"Uh, come in. Let me get my purse." She turned quickly before she liquefied right on her doorstep and hoped that she wouldn't topple over on her sky-scraper heels.

Maurice followed her inside. She could feel him behind her.

"Can I get you anything before we leave?"

"No. Thanks."

She picked up her purse from the counter and when she turned he was right there, right on top of her.

She drew in a sharp breath. In her heels she was almost eye-to-eye with him. She could clearly see the flecks of cinnamon in his eyes, the rich smooth-ness of his dark skin, the way the tiny waves in his hair looked like bands of silk.

He reached out a long, slender finger and stroked the line of her jaw, so featherlight it could have been her imagination. The corner of his mouth quirked ever so slightly.

"Ready?"

She blinked out of her trance. "Yes."

He took a step back.

Layla recovered her equilibrium and walked to-ward the door. Once outside she gulped in a cleans-ing breath of air to clear her head.

"My car is parked by the main entrance," he said.

"Okay." They continued along the path to the front of the property. "Where are we going?"

"B. Smith. I hope you like Southern food."

She perked up. "B. Smith is great." She looked across at him and smiled and her insides unfurled when he smiled right back.

He opened her door and helped her in before rounding the front of the car and getting behind the wheel of the silver gray Audi A8. The car oozed luxury with plush leather seats that she would give up her queen-sized bed to sleep on. The console looked like something from NASA, and when he started the engine, the car literally purred.

"Buckle up."

She did as instructed while he pressed a button to retract the sunroof.

The breeze blowing off the Sound was balmy and the sun was beginning to set wrapping the East Coast in that twilight world of the surreal.

Layla rested her head against her high seat back and took in the sights as the car made its way down the narrow streets. Maurice pressed another button and they were surrounded by the soothing voice of Kem.

"I love this CD," she said.

"So do I. I've played it so many times, I've had to replace it twice."

Layla laughed. "You too!"

He turned to her and dazzled her with a smile that filled her soul.

"I haven't had some good soul food in a while,"

he said as he turned onto the road that led to the main part of town.

"Neither have I now that I think about it. The neighborhood that I'm in has every kind of food you can imagine from every hamlet across the globe, but soul food is scarce."

"Where do you live?"

"In the West Village. And you?"

"Fort Greene, in Brooklyn."

Her eyes widened in delight. "Really. I love it over there."

"Do you? Well, maybe you'll come and visit sometime."

Her heart stilled. *Come and visit Fort Greene or come and visit him?* She didn't know what to say and thankfully she didn't have to respond. They pulled up in front of B. Smith's.

Maurice eased the car into a space and got out. He opened her door and extended his hand. His long, strong fingers wrapped around hers as he helped her from the car. Instead of stepping back to give her some room to exit, he pulled her right up to him.

Before she knew what was happening, his mouth possessed hers in a searing, hungry kiss that made her reel. And just as quickly as it had begun it was over and he released her onto her shaky legs.

"I've been wanting to do that since you opened your door." He brushed his thumb across her bottom lip then let it trail down to her collarbone. She shivered. "You have very kissable lips." He took a step back, crooked his arm in invitation.

Tentatively she slipped her arm through his and they walked together into the restaurant.

With all the conversations and activity buzzing around them, it gave Layla the opportunity to unscramble her thoughts and emotions. She couldn't figure Maurice out, she thought as she watched him mesmerize the waitress with that smile as he placed his order of ribs, collard greens and potato salad. Was he putting her on? Was he for real in his apparent attraction to her? Was this all some elaborate ruse to get back in her panties? She didn't know. How could she be sure of anything? Brent had done a real number on her sense of self, her sexuality, her desirability. Maybe she was simply too needy, still too raw and hurt and was getting mixed signals. She touched her finger to her lips that still felt the pull of his, held the sweet taste of him. She squirmed in her seat.

"Some wine or would you prefer your favorite?" he asked softly pulling her back into his magic web.

Layla rested her gaze on him. Don't over think this. See how it goes. It's only dinner. "Yes, wine, thanks."

Maurice signaled the waiter and requested a bottle of merlot.

"To being human," he said, lifting his glass in a toast.

Layla flushed. She lightly tapped her glass to his. "That remains to be seen," she tossed back and enjoyed the look of pleasant surprise that lit his eyes.

"Touché. What would I have to do *exactly* to show you the human side of Maurice Lawson?"

This was her chance to perhaps get beyond the imaginary wall that he'd set up around himself. She knew that there was so much more to him than sex in a bottle that needed to come with a warning label. But she knew that she would have to tread lightly.

She lifted her chin ever so slightly. "Well…you could start by telling me what you do when you're not here seducing unsuspecting masseuses."

He looked at her for a moment and then tossed his head back and laughed, a deep soul-stirring laugh that rumbled deliciously in her center. It was infectious. She couldn't help but join him.

His laughter slowly diminished but the soft smile remained. "I'm a computer engineer consultant for lack of a better set of terms."

Layla took a sip of her wine. "Sounds impressive. What does it mean?"

He chuckled. "I get called in to evaluate systems, set them up, redesign them based on the needs of the organization."

"That must keep you busy."

He nodded and reached for his glass. He took a sip and set his glass back down. "It does. Busy enough."

"Is that what you went to school for?"

A shadow passed across his face. "No." He paused for a moment as if contemplating saying anything further. "I learned it in the Navy."

"Oh."

The waiter arrived with their food and Layla's stomach sang joyfully in response. She hadn't eaten since breakfast.

Maurice opened his linen napkin and spread it on his lap. Layla did the same.

"Now let's see if B. Smith's lives up to its reputation."

They dug in and for the first ten minutes the only sound between them was clinking forks and murmurs of delight.

Halfway through the meal, when their appetites were partially satiated, Maurice asked her how she'd gotten into the massage business.

She took a sip of wine to clear her palate. "Well, it was always a dream of mine to have my own business. I love the feeling of bringing comfort to others. I believe the touch has the ability to heal in many ways. It took me a while to finish all my classes so I worked as a journalist for a few years."

"Multitalented."

She smiled as her right brow lifted. "I suppose. So, I trained, learned everything that I could." Flashes of Brent raced through her head, halting her in mid-sentence.

Maurice tipped his head to the side, his expression questioning.

She reached for her wineglass and found it empty.

Maurice lifted the bottle and refilled her glass.

"Thank you," she murmured and took a hungry sip.

"That bad?"

Her eyes jumped to his face then darted away. "It was," she finally admitted. "Not all of it. Just the end."

"Bad endings tend to linger."

Her gaze rose and settled on his face. His expression told a hundred stories at once. All she wanted was one. The story of what happened to him.

"What was your bad ending?"

His jaw tightened. She watched his Adam's apple moved up and down as if the words wanted to get out but couldn't.

"Not very good dinner conversation," he said finally. "Let's leave it at that."

She pressed her lips together then turned her attention back to her remaining dinner. "So, when you are not out rewiring the world, what do you like to do?"

He chuckled, and she peeked up at him through her long lashes and the shadow was gone. Just like that. He was so unsettling.

"Believe it or not, I play piano. A group of us get

together to do a gig every now and then. Local stuff. At least we used to," he added as an afterthought.

"What?" She beamed at him. "Piano? You certainly have the fingers for it." And as soon as the words were out of her mouth she felt her entire body heat with the memory of what those long fingers had done to her body. He remembered too. She could see it in the darkening of his gaze. The air between them charged.

"Can I show you the dessert menu?" the waiter asked, appearing as if summoned by some unseen hand.

"Nothing for me," Maurice said, his voice thick.

Layla swallowed over the hot tight knot in her throat. "No. Thank you." She forced herself to look up at the waiter to break the spell between her and Maurice.

"I'll take the check," Maurice said to the waiter but he never took his eyes off of Layla. The waiter handed him the check from his pad and took his credit card.

Layla was breathing too fast, but she couldn't slow it down, not with him staring at her as if *she* was dessert. There was a lusty hunger in his eyes that made the hairs on the back of her neck prickle. She shifted ever so slightly in her seat to relieve the building pressure between her thighs.

Layla made her mouth work. "How long have you played?" she asked in a whisper thin voice.

"Since I was a kid. My mother thought it would keep me out of trouble. Piano lessons every Wednesday and Saturday." He chuckled lightly at the distant memory.

She tried to imagine him as a little dark-eyed boy, propped up on a stool to reach the keys. The vision made her smile.

"All the lessons must have paid off. I guess you had to give it up when you went into the Navy," she said tentatively.

"Not entirely. When we did have a chance to go on leave or blow off some steam, I always tried to get in some time to play. It relaxes me."

"So. you picked it right back up…since you've been home."

He shrugged and looked into the depths of his wineglass.

"I'd love to hear you play sometime."

His gaze slowly moved to hers.

The waiter returned with his receipt and credit card.

"Ready?" he asked effectively halting that last line of conversation.

Was that another land mine that she'd stepped on?

Maurice rose slowly from his seat. She watched his mouth tighten as he stood. He straightened and reached for his cane.

She started to get up, to keep him from having to go through the ordeal of helping her from her seat when she could see that he was in pain. But the dark look of warning that he threw at her rooted her to her seat.

He took her arm and she slowly stood. "I'm not a cripple," he hissed from between his teeth. Fury and something she couldn't describe hovered in his eyes. *Shame?*

Layla opened her mouth to protest but she was already being ushered outside. He wordlessly led her around to the passenger side and opened her door.

Her whole body jerked when he slammed his door. She folded her arms tightly around her waist. She could feel her temper rising, bubbling like a pot of water turned on high. She whirled toward him.

"I don't know what your issues are, and quite frankly, right now I don't give a damn. Maybe you need to have a list of acceptable topics that your twisted personality is willing to discuss. You're a miserable, hurtful man who acts like the whole world is out to pity you. And you know what, I do. Not because of your injury. That's your issue. I pity you because you want to wallow in your misery and you'll always be alone if you do. And that's what's sad." Her chest heaved with the effort of her tirade and her pulsed pounded. "Take me home."

She swung away from him and turned her face to the window, biting on her bottom lip to keep from crying.

Maurice didn't utter a word. He turned on the car, backed out of the space and started back.

Layla didn't even comprehend that they'd returned until felt her door being opened. Her head jerked upward. Maurice was standing over her with his hand extended. She clasped her purse in her left hand, ignored his, got out of the car and brushed by him.

She stormed off down the path to her cottage.

"Layla. Wait."

Her heart pounded. She kept walking.

"I can't run after you."

The words stuttered her steps. She slowed, stopped and then turned around. Seeing him standing there, silhouetted against the backdrop of moonlight, magnified how incredibly hurt and alone he was. Her heart constricted.

"You can walk to me, though," she said with a lift of her chin.

He started coming toward her, and she felt like she was in one of those scenes from a romance movie where the hero comes home to his lady love. And then he was standing in front of her, and she was thankful for her heels that gave her the height to meet him.

His hand slid through her hair, clasping her behind her head. His eyes were on fire and they seared her skin as they grazed across her face.

"Show me how to be different," he said on a ragged whisper. "Tell me how to reconcile my two worlds. Teach me what you know about healing, because I'm all messed up inside."

Her throat squeezed and a tear spilled down her cheek. She took the hand that held her head and brought it to her side and led him into her cottage.

Chapter 13

The door shut behind them. Layla turned and stared into his eyes. She leaned up a bit and touched her lips to his and felt the vibration of his moan against her mouth. His arm snaked around her waist and her lips parted.

His tongue invaded her mouth, toyed with her, stoked her fire, and she eagerly returned the pleasure. This time it was Layla that eased away. She cupped his face in her hands.

"You're not going to use your incredible sex appeal to distract me. Not this time."

Maurice grinned. "I'm losing my charms already?"

She took his hand. "Come. Let's sit."

Maurice made himself comfortable on the couch. Layla stood in front of him. He reached out and clasped her thighs. His thumbs traced the soft insides and she shuddered. His hands moved up under her short dress, and suddenly she gripped his wrist with a strength that surprised them both.

She shook her head slowly back and forth and stepped out of his grasp. "I have the fixing for a mojito. Want one?"

Maurice leaned back. Absently he rubbed his injured leg. "Sure."

She whirled away and sauntered over to the small kitchen area. She could feel Maurice's eyes on her and she took full advantage. She stretched to reach the bottle and mojito mix in the cabinet and bent low to get the ice from the bottom drawer freezer. Within moments her favorite beverage was whirling in the blender.

She poured them into two large goblets and returned to the couch. She handed Maurice his glass and sat down beside him, then took off her shoes and tucked her leg beneath her. She angled her body to face him. "To healing," she said.

Maurice paused a moment and then touched his glass to hers. "Healing."

Layla took a long, cooling swallow. She was still unsure of what limits Maurice would throw in her way. Although he'd agreed to a truce of sorts and accepted his awfulness, he'd done it before. She'd been taken in before by his charm, by the carnal sensuality that seeped from his pores. She couldn't let him get the upper hand again. He was a man used to issuing orders and having them obeyed and that trait obviously spilled over into his everyday life. She drew in a breath of resolve.

"One of the first things that I learned about the healing power of touch was that both the giver and the receiver had to open themselves fully, release themselves of everything except the moment, the sensation of touch. The giver's mind must be clear so as not to transmit any of their negative energy to the receiver."

"I've had all kinds of massages, therapy, heat, cold treatment, pain pills…you name it." He sighed heavily. "They barely worked. But you…" His gaze connected with hers and she instantly felt that pull again.

"Maybe it was the first time you really allowed yourself to let go of the pain. When you do, the relief will come." Her eyes skimmed over his face that looked back at her with a mixture of awe and skepticism. She hesitated, mentally debated on how far she should go. "You're holding on to more than physical pain," she said slowly. She waited to gauge his reaction. "Whatever you have buried inside is more painful than the injury to your leg."

He looked away. Her pulse quickened but no emotional land mines blew up in her face. At least not yet.

Maurice draped his arm along the length of the

couch. "You seem to have the superpowers to see inside my dark soul," he said in a mocking tone. "What about you? What lies beneath all the loveliness?"

Layla picked up her drink. She brought the glass to her lips. "Okay. Quid pro quo. I tell something, you tell me something. Fair enough?"

He studied her for a moment. "You're serious?"

"Very."

His eyes registered amusement. He chuckled. "All right. Ladies first." His mouth hinted at a smile.

She lifted a finger. "But each revelation has to be of equal value."

His brow rose. "Meaning?"

"Meaning, if I confess that I attempted suicide you can't come back and with, you're allergic to ice cream."

Maurice let out a deep chuckle. "Fair enough. And one more caveat."

"Yes?"

"I get to call a halt."

Layla considered this a moment. In the corner of her mind she understood that even though he was giving in a little, he wasn't going to turn over all control. If she intended to make whatever this thing was work at all, she was going to have to meet him halfway.

"Fair enough," she finally said. She folded her hands on her lap. "My middle name is Marie," she said to break the confession ice.

That brought a smile to his face. "And my middle name is David."

"Maurice David Lawson." She smiled. "Has a nice ring to it. I'm an only child."

"So am I," he returned

Layla twisted her lips in thought. "I have a degree in journalism, but I don't really like it."

"I got my degree in the Navy like I mentioned before. I dropped out of college."

"Why?"

His gaze slid to hers. "Questions are part of the quid pro quo?"

"Hmm, we can adjust the rules as we go," she hedged.

"Then there's no point in having rules."

She crossed her legs and felt the heat of his gaze run along her limbs. "Point taken." She paused. "I grew up in Brooklyn, New York. I've lived there most of my life. When I graduated from college I moved to the West Village."

"Louisiana. My family is from Baton Rouge."

Her heart thumped. The family line had been crossed.

"Are they still there?"

It was as if a veil lowered over his face. The light in his eyes dimmed. He reached for his glass and took a long swallow and then another like he was fortifying himself.

"I suppose. I haven't spoken with them in years," he finally said, as he gazed off into the distance.

She desperately wanted to ask him why, but he'd put the brakes on questions. She tried another approach. "Too bad family can't be like friends. You can pick your friends, but not your family."

"The few friends that I do have make up for the family that I don't."

Now they were getting somewhere. "I have some great friends, too. Desiree for one. We've been friends since college. And Melanie and I are god-sisters."

"Well connected."

"Yeah. Desi is how I wound up here. Made me an offer I couldn't refuse," she said in a bad Marlon Brando impersonation.

That brought his devastating smile back. "Don't give up your day job."

Layla giggled.

He stroked her cheek with the tip of his finger. Her breath caught.

"I like hearing you laugh." His voice dropped an octave and settled in that place deep in her belly. "You should do it more often."

"So should you. You have a wonderful smile."

The corner of his mouth lifted. "Rule change."

"Rule change?"

"Yes. I want to ask you a question."

"Sure. But only if I get to ask you one."

He nodded in agreement.

She folded her arms and waited.

"Why did you leave after…?"

Layla's face heated. She looked away and shifted in her seat. "Wasn't expecting that," she murmured.

"Is that your final answer?" he asked, his tone teasing.

She pressed down a smile then looked into his eyes. "Scared I suppose."

"Of what?"

She turned her head away. "Of…what you would think. Of not understanding how I'd done something like that…"

He studied her expression, then took his finger, tucked it beneath her chin and lifted it. "I thought it was wonderful. I thought you were wonderful. And I don't know why I did it either, other than I wanted you in a way that I've never wanted a woman before. It was a need, like breathing."

She couldn't believe what she was hearing. Her pulse raced and her thoughts were so scrambled she couldn't respond.

Maurice jerked his head away. He put his glass on the coffee table, braced his hand on the arm of the couch and pushed up into a standing position. His facial muscles flexed. He reached for his cane.

"Wait. What are you doing?" She jumped up from her seat.

"This is why I don't do…this." He waved his hand in the air. A deep line intersected his brow.

"Do what?" she demanded, following him to the door.

"All this revelation B.S. I get enough of that with my shrink."

Layla halted in midstep.

His head swung in her direction, his face a hard mask. He tapped his temple with his forefinger. "Enough of being analyzed. I am the way I am because of my family and because of what I saw out there. What I did out there in those mountains. The bodies that were left behind! And those are things that all the psych talk and touchy-feely chat aren't going to change."

He pulled the door open.

"Go ahead, run! That's what you're really good at." He stopped. "You play tough guy, but you're a coward. Afraid to face the things you fear most."

"And what the hell is that supposed to mean?" he said between clenched teeth.

Her own anger flared. She propped her hands on her hips. "Exactly what I said. It's easy for you to hide behind your big planes and giant ships and orders and directions, but when you strip that all away, whenever anyone gets close to seeing behind the armor, you run. Just like you're doing now. Like you did earlier." Her chest heaved.

"Like you did?" he asked, his voice gentler, his point hitting home.

Layla drew in a breath. "Yes, but at least I was woman enough to admit it."

The hard line around his mouth softened. He turned halfway toward her. "Yeah, you were." His eyes moved slowly over her determined expression.

"Why do you care?" he asked, and the look in his dark eyes squeezed her heart.

She stepped toward him. She covered his hand that held the doorknob. "I don't know," she softly confessed. "Maybe because I know what it's like to run from the things that hurt you, that you're afraid will hurt you again." She waited a moment before reopening the gates of their tacit quid pro quo agreement. "He hurt me," she said quietly. "I thought he loved me. But he couldn't have. Not after what he did to me." She lowered her head to shield him from the memories that hovered behind her eyes.

"My uncle was responsible for my father's suicide. He's never been held accountable." His jaw clenched.

Layla stared into his eyes. She held her breath.

"I was responsible for the deaths of two of my men. And I live with that every day."

Layla held her hand out to him. Tentatively, he placed his hand in hers.

Chapter 14

The air remained charged between them. Layla watched the tight nerves jump beneath his smooth skin. His large hands curled into fists. His jaw flexed as if he was chewing back the words he wanted to hurl across the room.

All of that contained anger and hurt was volatile and as poisonous to his body and spirit as an illness. It was eating him from the inside out and Layla knew that until he fully addressed it, the pain wasn't going anywhere.

"You're holding on to so much blame and anger," she said softly.

Maurice jerked his gaze in her direction. Layla held her breath. He studied her for a moment. "What happened between you and…the guy?" Maurice asked.

Deflection. He was real good at that. Layla curled herself into the couch and half turned toward him. "Brent." She breathed deeply. "We met at a club. Hit it off. I was cautious at first, but he won my trust. He was attentive, fun, he had his own business, one that I was interested in as well. He took me under his wing…so to speak." She made a sound of disgust in her throat. "We got involved and it got serious. At least I thought so." She reached for her glass and took a sobering sip of her mojito.

Maurice's expression softened. "You said I'm holding on to a lot of blame." He inhaled deeply. "It's all I have left," he confessed.

Layla settled her focus on him and waited, hopeful that her revelation would open the door for his.

He stared off into a place that she could not go, back to that night. The plan had been in place for months. The teams had met repeatedly with the Secretary of Defense and the President. Every eventuality was taken into account. The two teams were handpicked. The intel they had was verified and re-verified. The only variable was the weather. There had to be enough cloud cover, but not enough to hinder visibility and the mission.

His was the command leader for his team of five SEALs, men that he'd trained and worked with over the years. They trusted each other with their lives.

They trusted him and he'd destroyed that trust when their Black Hawk went down in the mountains of Afghanistan, two miles off of their target.

He had to look into the eyes of his buddys' wives and families and see their pain. And there was nothing he could do. He couldn't even admit that he was part of the operation. Top Secret. No one blamed him. He'd been cleared of all wrongdoing by the Navy but it wasn't enough. It would never be enough. No one seemed to understand that.

"I've tried to let go," he said, his voice barely audible.

Layla took his hand and dared to curl up next to him. Maurice tentatively draped his arm around her shoulder and pulled her close.

"You'll let go when you are ready." She lightly squeezed his hand. "You'll forgive yourself when you're ready." She looked up at him.

He leaned down and gave her a feather soft kiss and hugged her close.

They sat together, quietly. The only sound was the distant crash of the waves against the shore. A wave of contentment flowed through Layla. She closed her eyes, lulled by the steady beat of his heart and his tender stroking of her hair.

Maurice gazed down as the comforting arms of sleep gathered Layla in its embrace. The contours of her face softened and her supple skin glowed from within. The tranquility that radiated from her beat in time with her heart and moved through his limbs, suffusing him in a sense of peace that was ethereal. He closed his eyes and breathed in the peace, the feeling of calm that washed over him with every gentle breath that she took.

To feel like this, if only for a little while, was worth the pain it took to get here.

Layla felt warm, almost too warm. She stirred. Her eyes fluttered open and the world came into focus.

Maurice's arm was wrapped securely around her and her head was pressed against his chest. His even breathing matched hers in soothing harmony. The cocooned feeling beckoned her back to the womb of sleep.

Maurice shifted, a soft hum of contentment vibrated in his chest. Layla smiled.

"You awake?"

Layla lifted her head to find him staring down at her. "Kind of." She pulled herself into an upright position. "I didn't even realize I'd fallen asleep. Some hostess, huh?" She pushed her hair away from her face and was thankful for the lack of light. She must look a hot mess.

Maurice stilled the hand that she was threading through her hair. "You look beautiful," he said softly.

In the light from the moon his gaze traveled slowly across her face. Her pulse quickened.

"I should get going."

"It is late," she said on a hushed breath.

Maurice's finger trailed down the side of her face and along her jaw. He brushed his thumb across her bottom lip and thrilling shivers scooted up her spine. Her breath hitched and then he was out of focus as his mouth covered hers.

Layla sunk into the sweet demand of his mouth, giving him as much as he gave her. The hard cords of his arm snaked around her, stealing her breath away.

Maurice moaned against her lips. His tongue played with the tip of hers before invading her mouth in slow, tantalizing thrusts.

His fingertips played along her spine, down the small of her back, before cupping her round bottom and gently squeezing. Her inner thighs quivered.

"I should go," he whispered raggedly against her lips.

"Yes," she sighed, as his head dipped down and his tongue teased that soft spot along her collarbone. Her body shivered with need, arching closer.

His hand slipped under her dress in a stealth motion, worthy of a Navy SEAL. He unfastened her bra and filled his hands with the fullness of her breasts.

Maurice lifted the lightweight fabric of her bra and pressed his face against her firm pillows. Layla moaned as her body flooded with heat. He teased a nipple between his fingertips, until that stood up firm and full, before taking one and then the other into his mouth, laving them with his tongue, sucking them between his lips until she was ready to explode.

With shaky fingers she unbuttoned his shirt, pushed it away from his chest and inhaled the essence of him that made her heart rush.

"It's late," she said breathlessly as she unbuckled his belt.

"I know. Raise your arms."

She did and he lifted her dress over her head and tossed it to the floor. Then added her lacy bra to it.

Layla could not control the tremors of desire that fluttered through her. With his every touch, every kiss, the flame that he'd lit in the pit of her belly bloomed.

"Stand up," he said thickly.

She blinked in confusion, but slowly stood.

Maurice hooked his fingers into the band of her panties and slowly slid them down her hips, placing tiny hot kisses along her exposed flesh.

She was trembling all over and felt as if she was ready to melt into the pool of clothing.

Maurice braced her hips with his large hands. His thumbs were low on either side of her pelvis. He stroked her there, so lightly that it could have been her imagination if it were not for the jolts of electricity that shook her like a taser.

His fingers continued to tease her, moving closer to the apex of her sex. She was wet with need. His thumb brushed across her pulsing clit. Her body jerked and she cried out. He did it again and again, building the rhythm and intensity.

By instinct, Layla rocked her hips against the sweet torture, eager for more. Her fingertips dug into his shoulders.

When Maurice's wet tongue stroked her throbbing bud, her knees wobbled and white hot lights flashed behind her lids.

"Ohhhh…"

He gripped her tighter to keep her upright and continued to feast, taking long swipes, quick flicks, alternating back and forth, slower, faster until she was a vessel of pure, trembling sensation. And when she knew she could take no more, and whimpered for release, he slipped his finger inside of her, swirling it gently around and then in and out and she exploded. The force of her climax roared through her with the speed of light, spinning her like clothes on the line during a cyclone. It rose and fell and rose again until she collapsed in his arms. Spent.

Maurice gathered her to him and held her until her body quieted and her breathing slowed. Somehow, he picked her up and slowly walked with her into her bedroom, all semblance of pain gone from his leg. Tenderly he laid her down and pulled the sheet up over her. She sighed softly and reached for him in the dark.

He leaned down and gently pressed his lips to hers and then he was gone.

As much as he wanted to stay with Layla, wake up with her, make love with her, he couldn't. He closed his cottage door behind him. She was doing something to him, something beyond the undeniable sexual attraction that sparked between them. She was finding her way beneath his skin. She was getting into his head, forcing him to confront the dark part of him that needed to stay buried, answer questions that he didn't have the answers for. He wasn't ready for what she needed. And he wasn't sure if he would ever be.

He fell across the bed and stared up at the ceiling. Layla's face floated above him until he finally drifted off to sleep.

Layla blinked against the soft light that filtered in between the curtained window. She stretched like a satisfied cat, purring softly then suddenly leaped up. She was completely naked. She listened for sounds of Maurice. Nothing. She turned, checked the space beside her and knew instantly that no one had slept there.

What the… She tossed the sheet aside, scrambled out of bed and darted to the front. No sign of Maurice. She heaved an exasperated sigh, totally unable to put together what had gone wrong. Was he just toying with her? Was she so needy that all it took was a few hot kisses and she was putty?

She bit down on her lip. Once again Maurice Lawson had successfully managed to make her feel like crap. "Damn it!" She spun away and stormed off to the bathroom. What she needed right then was to wash away every single trace of Maurice from her skin, even if she couldn't wash him out of her head.

Bathed and wrapped in a towel, Layla padded into her bedroom. No matter how hard she tried to keep them at bay her eyes continued to fill with tears. She felt so, so…her heart hurt. Her heart actually hurt. She swiped the tears away from her eyes.

She wasn't progressive minded like Mel and free-spirited like Desi. They believed that if a woman had needs and found a man who could meet them it didn't have to be about "forever." But she couldn't sleep with a man only to fulfill a physical need— not that they actually slept together—it had to mean something. She supposed that was her Achilles' heel. But she couldn't change that part of herself. It mattered. When was she going to stop making the same mistakes and stop falling for men that meant her no good?

She wiped her eyes again with the back of her hand then stopped at the sound of knocking. Frowning, she tightened the belt on her robe and walked to the front door.

She pulled the curtain aside by the front door window and her heart thudded. She swiped at her eyes again and ran her hands across her hair in a useless attempt at taming it, then opened the door.

"I was hoping you hadn't left for the spa yet," Maurice said. He held up two white paper bags in one hand and a cardboard tray with two steaming cups of coffee in the other.

Layla's throat constricted with emotion. She didn't know if she wanted to cry, scream or leap into his arms. She swallowed over the knot in her throat. "Come in," she said softly and stepped aside.

Chapter 15

Maurice set the bags and the coffee on the island counter and took a seat on the stool while Layla took out two plates from the overhead cabinet.

Her pulse raced like crazy. A million thoughts galloped through her head. Why was he here? Did she overreact this morning? Maybe he'd only been gone shortly before she awoke. Was there an apology coming? WTH?

She swung toward him. "Why did you leave?" she demanded.

Maurice blinked in surprise before looking away. He studied the coffee cup then he steepled his fingers at his chin and looked her solidly in the eye.

"Thought it was the best thing to do," he finally said. A faint look of amusement played around his lips.

Her mouth opened and closed. The words wouldn't form. Slowly she shook her head, turned toward the drawers and took out forks and knives. She slapped them down on the counter and felt like tossing his plate across the room.

Her wide eyes cinched into two tight lines. "You thought it was the best thing to do?" she sputtered incredulously. Her voice rose an octave with each word. "I…why…what would make you think that? Why would you think it would be all right?"

"I'm here now."

Her head nearly snapped off of her neck. Her mouth dropped open. She blinked rapidly and the words tumbled over each other in a rush. "No you're not. You're not here for a hot second longer than it's going to take for you to get your arrogant ass out of my kitchen," she yelled, her arm straight as an arrow pointing toward the door.

Maurice pursed his lips.

"And take your peace offering breakfast with you!"

"You really want me to go?" he asked quietly, slowly coming to his feet.

"Get out. Right now." She was so angry she was shaking.

Maurice came around the counter.

"What are you doing?" She backed up. "Stay the hell away from me."

Maurice kept coming until he'd back her up against the refrigerator.

Layla's chest heaved. "Stay away from me, Maurice," she ground out.

He cupped her chin. "You sure?" He flexed his pelvis against her and the hard rise of his blooming erection pressed into her stomach.

She drew in a sharp breath. Her eyes widened.

"I left last night," he began and then kissed her behind her ear. She gasped. "Because I had to." He ran his tongue along her collarbone. The fingers of his left hand played with the sash of her robe. He placed a muscled leg between her thighs, coaxing them open. He tugged and the sash came loose. His dark gaze seared across her exposed flesh.

The mixture of anger, fear and need converged into a whirling ball of unbridled lust. Her breathing escalated and her skin tingled with heat. Her palms were pressed flat against the fridge, as much to claim any cold that it might emit as to keep her hands off of him.

He brushed a thumb across her exposed nipple and she barely bit back the whimper.

"I had to leave," he continued as he cupped the weight of her breast in his palm. He lowered his head. She tried to jerk away but he had her pinned to the hard surface of the fridge. The most she could do was turn her face away from his kiss. "Because if I didn't…" he flicked his tongue across her nipple, "I would have made crazy, sweet love to you…" he sucked the hard nub into his mouth and released it… Her body throbbed. "…all night long."

He took her mouth then, possessed it, capturing and savoring its sweetness. His teeth grazed her bottom lip before he slipped his tongue inside her mouth.

Layla moaned. The icy front that she tried to put up melted away and the mix of his heat and her liquid desire steamed the room.

She arched her neck to give him full access and clasped the back of his head to hold him in place.

"That. Is. Not. A. Reason," she said, hot and breathless.

Slowly Maurice raised his head from the tender cord of her neck. He looked into her eyes. The corner of his sweet mouth lifted ever so slightly. His dark eyes sparkled.

"All right. I'll tell you." He took a step back and kept his eyes locked on her. "I didn't have any protection."

Layla blinked in disbelief. She lightly flung her head back and forth then focused on Maurice. "You're serious? You wanted to stay and make love to me, but you didn't because you didn't have protection?"

He nodded slowly.

She pushed out a breath and shrugged out of her robe. It dropped to the floor. "What about now?"

Maurice ran his tongue across his bottom lip. A dangerous smile reached his eyes. He stuck his hand into his pocket, pulled out two small packets and held them up in front of her.

A slow seductive smile moved across Layla's mouth. "I think you're going to need more than two, Mr. Lawson."

They tumbled into Layla's bedroom in a tangle of arms and legs and mouths, and fell onto the bed amidst sighs, groans and wet kisses.

Layla grabbed the hem of Maurice's white T-shirt and tugged it over his head. His mouth and tongue were everywhere, stoking her heated skin. With one pull, the drawstring in the waistband of his gray sweatpants was loose and access to the treasure that she sought was fingertips away. Her hungry hand wrapped around him and the sound from the recesses of his throat was the low growl of a tiger. She vibrated with it like a guitar string that had been plucked.

Maurice flipped their side-by-side positions and pinned Layla beneath him. He cupped her face in his hands. Her lashes fluttered. He braced his weight on his arms.

"I've been thinking about this all night," he whispered. "So, I hope your clients don't mind if you're a little late for work."

Slowly he lowered his head and kissed her with such tenderness that her insides sang. She linked her fingers behind his head and pulled him deeper into the kiss, taking his tongue into her mouth, savoring his taste, doing a slow dance.

Maurice's hands and mouth moved in harmony along her body, igniting every inch until she was a bed of sensation.

"You're overdressed for the occasion," she managed.

Maurice grinned. He raised up and pulled off his sweatpants and boxers. "Better?"

Layla rose up on her knees and scooted closer. "Very," she purred, running her short nails across his broad, bare chest then slowly downward toward the thin trail of silky hair that led to a world of ecstasy.

She encircled his erection in her hand, stunned again by the satin feel of him wrapped around rock hard power. Maurice groaned deep in his throat as she began to stroke him up and down, intermittently giving a little squeeze. She leaned forward while continuing to stroke him and flicked her tongue across his nipple then nipped it ever so lightly. His erection pulsed in response. She did it again and again, and the pulse grew more intense until it beat like a heart. Maurice sucked in air from between clenched teeth. He gripped her wrist.

"Enough," he ground out and pushed her onto her back before she could blink. He knelt between her parted thighs then ran his hands slowly up her legs, behind her knees and down the inside of her thighs.

Her stomach fluttered and her breathing rapidly escalated. His fingers grazed the eager lips of her sex and her hips rose in response. He cupped her with his large hand and ran the pad of his thumb across her awakened clit, teasing and taunting it out of its protective sheath.

Layla gasped in pleasure. She bent her knees to give herself more leverage and pressed against his palm wanting more, and he gave it to her in maddeningly slow increments until she was wild and whimpering, held captive on the precipice of release.

Layla's eyes fluttered open at the sound of something ripping. Maurice had the condom packet between his teeth. He pulled the condom out and tossed the packet on the floor. She followed his every move while he erotically put on a condom.

He placed the thin rubber on the moist tip and rolled it down his considerable length. She reached for him the instant he was done.

"No." He shook his head slowly as he clasped her hands, linking his fingers between hers then coming slowly forward until he was inches above her and her arms were stretched and pinned over her head.

"Spread your legs, and bend your knees," he said, his tone hard and soft at once. "More," he hissed until her feet nearly reached either edge of the bed. He pressed the pulsing head of his erection against her wet opening. She lifted her hips in response and he pulled away.

"Don't move." He pressed down again, pushing in a little further this time, just beyond her opening.

"Ohhh…"

"Ssssh." He pulled out.

Her limbs trembled.

Maurice eased in again…and out…and deeper… deeper…almost all the way…

Layla cried out and he pulled out. Her eyes flew open and she saw the wicked light of lust and something else in his dark eyes, and she realized that he could easily torment her like this for as long as he chose and the only way to find relief was to follow his commands. She was trapped in a vortex of sensation. The sounds that she couldn't make aloud played a maddening symphony in her head. Her body that instinctively needed to respond to what he was doing to her was held motionless, which only elevated the torrent of sensations that ripped through her, rising and falling and rising until she was sure she would burst.

Maurice pushed halfway inside of her and slowly rotated his hips. She bit down on her lip to keep from screaming, just as his mouth came down and captured a hard nipple that was thrust up at him. He sucked ever so gently while he wound his hips in a slow circle. Her fingertips dug into his hands. Tears hung in the corners of her eyes.

"I want you," he murmured between the heavy pillows of her breasts. "So bad…" His voice sounded choked.

She needed to touch him, but he had her hands pinned. She needed to give herself to him, but he would deny her satisfaction if she moved. It was an incomprehensible turn-on that aroused and scared her.

"I want you," he ground out again and thrust hard and deep all the way inside her, forcing the air out of her lungs. He plunged into her again and stars exploded behind her lids. Again and again. "I want you," he kept repeating over and over with each thrust and circle of his hips.

Her entire body shook.

"Put your legs around my back," he commanded.

She was nearly limp with need and barely able to lift her legs up to wrap them around his back. She locked her heels, binding him to her and the sensation of him pressed so hard against her swollen clitoris forced a strangled cry from her throat.

But this time he didn't pull away and her hungry hot, wet tunnel eagerly wrapped around him and her mind-altering orgasm began at the tips of her fingers. It moved down her outstretched arms, across her taut breasts, then up from the soles of her feet, the back muscles of her calves, the softness of her inner thighs and settled deep in her womb, then like a bomb erupted in white hot light and took everything with it. And Maurice poured the essence of his hopes, fears, and happiness deep within her.

Chapter 16

By degrees their breathing returned to somewhat normal. Layla lay spooned with Maurice, her back to his front, still trying to come to grips with the awesomeness of the experience. Even as a former journalist she was without words. There was nothing worthy of describing what he had done and how he had made her feel. A delicious shiver rippled up her spine.

Maurice drew her closer and kissed the top of her head. He managed to grab the edge of the sheet and cover her and then returned his hand possessively between her legs. His other arm was wrapped around her, his palm splayed across her left breast where he intermittently gave a tender squeeze or brushed his thumb across her sensitive nipple that shot electricity straight to her center.

"How much time do you have?" he whispered into her ear.

She felt his erection press and grow against her. She moaned softly. "Not long."

"I promise I won't be long then."

As if she weighed no more than a loaf of bread, he turned her onto her belly and rose up on his knees to roll on the last condom.

Maurice slid his arm under her stomach and pulled her up so that her luscious behind was high in the air and her wet opening an easy mark.

He rained hot kisses along her spine and taunted her wet cat with his fingers until she literally purred while she gyrated her hips in a sexy tease. His muscled arm tightened around her waist holding her immobile and in one swift motion he thrust into her, pushing a cry of agony and ecstasy from her lips.

He held her firmly in his grasp as he plunged in and out of her, gritting his teeth as the sensations built, filling him, stiffening him until he felt as if he would snap if relief didn't come soon. Faster, deeper, harder he moved, seeking the hidden treasure buried within her.

Layla's moans grew in intensity. Desperately she wanted to move against him so that he could hit that spot, and as if he read her mind and body, he loosened his hold. Freed, she lifted her rear higher.

Maurice let out a low groan. His thighs shook. She felt like a missile was moving in and out of her. Her orgasm was building. She felt it everywhere. Her temples pounded. The sounds of Maurice's ragged groans fueled her. She wound her hips hard and fast and banged against him. Their worlds converged and exploded.

Layla's legs were so weak, she could barely walk Maurice to the door. Her insides still fluttered and her cat kept winking, making it hard to concentrate. Talk about aftershock.

"Guess I owe you lunch since we missed breakfast," he said.

She looked up at him standing in her doorway. His dark eyes had a lazy, satisfied expression.

"I'll hold you to that."

He leaned down and kissed her softly on the lips and then tenderly stroked her cheek. "Thank you," he whispered. He turned from her and walked away, his limp barely noticeable.

It took a moment for Layla to snap out of her daze and close the door. Slowly she turned away, forced herself to think about what she needed to do. It was nearly ten and her first client was scheduled for ten-thirty. What she really wanted to do was crawl back in bed, sink into her pillow, inhale Maurice's scent on her sheets then curl around the memories of her mind-blowing morning. She blew out a breath of amazement, padded back to her bedroom to get dressed while every sinew in her body hummed a little tune.

Maurice reclined on a lounge chair on his back porch, sipped some orange juice and enjoyed the view of the ocean. A soft smile rested peacefully on his expression. He felt good, really felt good. Humph, how long at it been since he'd been able to even imagine feeling good again?

For more than a decade his every action had been dictated by anger and hurt. His emotions were fueled by wanting others to feel the pain and the loss that he did when his father'd died. So, he'd joined the Navy in the hopes of traveling so far away from the things that were familiar that he would eventually forget them. But he didn't. So, he turned his anger and feelings of loss into training for the SEALs, rising up the ranks to lead a team of fearless men who were willing to risk anything for the mission.

It was enough for a while. Most days he was too busy to think, and at night too tired to dream—until that last mission. And it all came back, tenfold. But now he was unable to ever resume his place with the SEALs, the only outlet that had been the balm for his soul, had resuscitated and escalated the emotions that he'd kept at bay. Then he'd met Layla.

His cell phone vibrated and shimmied across the

glass table. He reached for it and half smiled when he saw the caller ID.

"Hey, Doc."

It took all Layla had to stay focused on her work. Every time she rubbed oil on her hands and placed them on waiting skin and tight muscles, her thoughts flew to Maurice and what he felt like beneath her fingertips. She could hear the sounds that he made as the heat and healing vibes from her transferred to him; the way his muscles tightened and eased. But OMG, what that man could do to her body…

"Finished?" her client murmured.

Layla blinked. *Damn*. She had totally zoned out. "Just a few more minutes." She drew in a shaky breath and put her all into finishing up.

Layla closed and locked the door behind her last customer. It was nearly two and her next client wasn't scheduled until three. She rolled her neck to loosen her stiff shoulders. Maurice said he owed her lunch. Her stomach fluttered with anticipation. But he didn't say where. Did he plan to stop by the spa or did he expect her to come by his place? Or did he even mean today?

She went about reorganizing the space and replacing towels and colleting used items for the laundry pick up. By the time she was done nearly an hour had passed and still no sign of Maurice.

Fine. He apparently didn't mean today. She took

a quick look around. Everything was in order. She got her purse from the desk drawer, locked up and headed over to the café to get something to eat.

Layla walked along the path leading to the main building and vaguely noticed two people standing near the slope leading to the beach. At first she thought nothing of it. But her chest tightened when she stopped and looked closer. It was Maurice and Kim Fleming. She had a grip on Maurice's arm and it was clear they were in a heated discussion. Then suddenly Kim spun away and ran in the direction of the beach. Maurice watched her go.

Layla's heart pounded. What was that about? She watched Maurice from her vantage point. He stood there, lowered his head a moment and then turned and walked away.

Chapter 17

He knew who she was the moment he'd set eyes on her that day in the spa. *Jason Fleming's wife*. He leaned his head back against the cushions of the couch and closed his eyes. His jaw tightened as images of Jason lying in that heap of rubble and hot twisted metal flashed in front of him. He should have left The Port then before she had a chance to put it together, but he'd stayed because of Layla.

When Kim confronted him on the slope he so wanted to tell her about that night, about what happened. But he was bound by secrecy, even now. So he'd lied. He told her that she was mistaken even as she insisted that she knew it was him from the photo of the team that her husband had once sent to her. She'd thought that her recollection was limited to his connection to Rafe. But then she'd put it all together. Jason had served with a Maurice Lawson. She'd looked through her cell phone at the photos that Jason had uploaded and although it wasn't crystal clear, she knew that it was Maurice.

"Were you with him on that mission?" she'd wanted to know. "Did he say anything? What happened that night?"

And like Judas, he'd denied everything, even after she begged him for the truth, a truth that haunted his every hour.

Desiree found Layla seated in a corner at the outdoor café.

"Hey, done for the day?"

Layla barely glanced up. She lifted her glass of iced tea and put it back down.

Desiree sat. "What's wrong?" She studied Layla's tight expression. Finally, Layla looked up.

"I saw something today."

Desiree frowned. "Something? Something like what?"

Layla pushed out a breath and told Desiree what she'd witnessed on the slope.

"It could have been anything," Desiree said, not too convincingly.

Layla's brow rose. "Anything like what?"

"Ask him, La. If it bothers you that much." She

reached across the table and covered Layla's hand with her own. "It's probably nothing. Maybe she was trying to make a play for him. Anyway, even if it was something, it's a moot point."

"Why is that?"

"She checked out about a half hour ago, anyway."

"Checked out? Was it sudden or…"

"Today was her last day. Nothing mysterious." She offered up a smile.

Layla looked away. "I wonder if he'll say anything to me about it," she murmured, half to herself.

"Sometimes, you have to pick your battles, La."

"There were signs with Brent," she quietly admitted.

Desiree flinched.

"I didn't want to see what was going on."

"Layla, what do you mean, what signs? We were all under the impression that it was sudden."

She slowly shook her head. She wrapped her fingers around her glass. "I didn't want to say anything to you and Mel."

"Why, sis?"

Layla glanced up from beneath her long lashes. "You and Mel had it all together; great lives, wonderful men, flourishing businesses, successful marriages. And my life was coming apart at the seams, one stitch at a time." She sputtered a derisive laugh.

"We're your friends, Layla. You could have told us what was going on." She squeezed Layla's hand.

"I know. I should have...I..." She pushed out a sigh. "Brent started staying at the spa later. We used to go out a lot. That started slowing down. And...he stopped...touching me."

"Oh, Layla..."

She sniffed and blinked back tears.

"You were going through all this alone?"

"It was so gradual that I almost didn't notice. And when I said anything, he'd tell me that I was blowing things out of proportion. He said he was trying to build the business, that he was tired...the list goes on. I didn't want to rock the boat so I tried not to press him. I tried not to make an issue of things. I tried not to ask too many questions." Her gaze rose to meet Desiree's. "That's why I can't let this go. I'm not going to be the same fool twice, Desi," she declared, her voice taking on strength.

"I hear you." She paused thoughtfully. "Then you need to talk to him. Clear the air."

Layla slowly nodded in agreement. "I intend to."

Desiree's cell phone rang. She dug her phone from her pants pocket. "It's Mel," she mouthed. "Hey, girl, what's up?...Okay. I'm here with Layla. Sure. Hold on a sec." She held the phone away from her mouth. "Mel wants me to come by later to talk about the party. You want to come? You should."

Layla nodded, yes.

"Layla is going to come, too. We'll be there around seven. Great. See you later." She disconnected the call and turned her focus on Layla. "Look, we'll have a girl's night, talk, have a few drinks, discuss the party and figure this Maurice Lawson thing out."

Layla leaned back in her seat. A shadow of a smile tugged the corners of her mouth. "Sounds like a plan."

Maurice took a slow and measured walk along the shore. After his talk with his therapist and then running into Kim, he needed to clear his head. He felt like two people wrestling for control in one body. A part of him was trapped in his past, trapped by dark emotions, trapped by pain and invested in disdain. The other part of him was filled with a glimmer of hope, a sliver of light, it teased him with what life would be like if he relinquished the burden of his mental and physical chains. Layla opened that door for him. She held the key to chains that bound him. When he was with her he understood how things could be, but to give in to those emotions would be to concede defeat. It would mean allowing the memory of his father to be forever tarnished by what his uncle had allowed to happen. It would mean absolving himself of his role in the deaths of his friends.

And he was not sure that he or his uncle deserved absolution or forgiveness.

He leaned down and picked up a seashell. The sand that coated it shone like flecks of diamonds in the late day sun. The soothing sound of the waves, the echoes of laughter and the caw of the seagulls all lent themselves to wash him in a feeling of calm. When he looked out beyond the horizon, it was a different life that he saw there. It wasn't the life that he'd lived for the past ten years. It was the life he could have had if things had not gone so terribly wrong.

He didn't want to go back to the way things were. He'd gotten a taste of how good things could be. He got to experience, once again, what it felt like to let go of all the hurt and anger and disappointment and feel real happiness. All the months of therapy had not done that, but Layla had.

That was yet another dilemma that he wrestled with—his feelings for Layla. Were they even real or merely a result of how she'd physically made him feel?

He pressed his cane down into the sand and allowed it to bare his weight. It was more than physical. He pushed out a long breath of acceptance. It was more than her ability to make his pain go away. And, for Maurice, that realization was more frightening than an unseen enemy.

Chapter 18

"You know I'm all for being up front," Melanie was saying as she set out a tray of baby quiche appetizers on the outdoor table. A warm breeze blew in off of the ocean. "I am a firm believer in knowing what's going on in a relationship...mine and everyone else's," she added with a laugh. "It may very well be nothing. But it will bug you until doomsday if you don't say anything. Let him tell you and then it's up to you to believe him or not." She reached for a quiche. "But that does not let you off the hook for not telling us what the hell that bastard Brent was doing."

Layla crossed her long legs and munched on her piece of quiche. "I know. Water under the bridge now."

"'Cause you know it wouldn't have taken any-thing out of me to make a little road trip to the city," Desiree said.

"Exactly. Pay Mr. Davis a little visit. Wake up and find a horse's head in his bed," Melanie said, doing a very bad job of looking the tough girl part with her expertly coiffed hair, perfectly applied makeup and designer attire.

Layla and Desiree burst out laughing, sputtering pieces of quiche.

"Mel, you are a fool," Layla managed. She reached for a napkin and wiped her mouth.

Melanie arched a brow and bit down on a grin. "You know I know people who know people. We can still get him put in a trunk somewhere, and Maurice too, if he doesn't act right. I don't care who his uncle is." She twisted her lush lips in annoyance.

"Stop, okay. Nobody is getting put in a trunk," Layla said over her giggles.

"Humph."

"Anyway...do you need me to do anything for the party?"

"Agree to let me introduce you to some of my very eligible bachelors that will be there."

Layla made a face. "Don't you think I have enough to deal with?"

"It will give Maurice something to think about if he sees another man interested in you."

"I'm not going to play games, Mel."

"Who said anything about playing games? I'm very serious. Maurice Lawson hasn't slipped a ring on your finger. He doesn't own you. And just because he turned your lights back on doesn't mean he's the only one who can."

"Mel!" Desiree chastised.

"What?" she asked wide-eyed. "It's the truth. He has to be more than good in bed. Can we all at least agree on that?" Layla and Desiree nodded in reluctance. "If you are even thinking about making a real commitment to that man, you are going to know him inside out. He's got to be up front with you and you with him. And then you both decide if you want to deal with what you've exposed."

"We have talked," Layla said. "His scars aren't only from his injury. They're deep and he's trying to find a way to deal with them."

Melanie picked up her wineglass and raised it to her lips. "If there is one thing that I learned over the years, from being in the matchmaking business, you can't fix a man. You can't turn a man into someone he has no intention of being, no matter how much they care about you and you care about them. There is only so much changing they will do. And if by some miracle they do, you realize that all the things you changed are the very things that drew you to them in the first place."

"So, what are you saying, Mel?"

"I'm saying, the scars, the baggage, the whatever,

are all a part of who Maurice is, who any of us are. If it's going to work it, will have to work with both parties accepting that, finding a way to make it work in spite of the imperfections. But you can't erase them. You simply can't."

Layla allowed room in her own muddied thoughts for Melanie's advice. Mel was always the straight shooter of the trio, Ms. No Nonsense and it never steered her wrong. But this time… She sipped her mojito. "So, how many people are you expecting for this shindig?"

Mel laughed. "In honor of Desiree and Lincoln I've kept my list to a modest fifty."

"Gee thanks," Desiree deadpanned. She turned to Layla. "Did you ever ask Maurice if he wanted to come?"

"No. I meant to but we always seem to get distracted." A wicked grin flickered on her lips.

"I think it'll be the perfect opportunity for me to check him out up close, and for you to see how he flows in the world."

"Before or after I ask him about Kim Fleming?"

Melanie leaned forward. "Everyone seems to be so much more agreeable *after* one of my parties. Besides, if he doesn't say what you want to hear, I don't want you to mope through the whole party. It will make it that much harder to get one of my eligibles interested in you."

"Mel! Enough of trying to set me up."

Melanie threw up her hand. "All right, all right. But just remember I have a fabulous track record." She glanced toward the doorway and her entire countenance became lit from within. "Just ask my sexy husband."

Claude strolled over, leaned down and placed a long, slow kiss on his wife's lips. "You ladies still plotting to take over the world?"

"Of course," Desiree said. "And it will be so smooth and well planned, you men won't even know what happened."

"Promises, promises," Claude said. He perched on the edge of Melanie's chair. "How are the party plans going?"

"Everything is set. I finalized everything with the caterer this morning and the entertainment manager."

"I can't thank you both enough for doing this for me and Lincoln."

"Mel doesn't need a reason for a party," Claude said. He gave her shoulder a loving squeeze.

"And there is never a better reason than to celebrate a successful relationship," she said, gazing lovingly up at her husband.

Claude leaned down and kissed her tenderly then sat up. "I will leave you ladies to continue doing what it is you do when men aren't around."

Desiree and Layla finger-waved as Claude walked back into the house.

"So…what *is* on the menu?" Desiree asked.

And the trio launched into the details of the up-coming party.

Maurice walked back from the beach with the intention of stopping by the spa, hoping to see Layla even though he knew it was beyond closing time. As he'd suspected, he found the spa closed up tight. He needed to speak to her. After his talk with his therapist and then seeing Kim there was so much he wanted to tell Layla. She had a way of making him see things that were right in front of him all the time, providing a kind of clarity that made the obstacles surmountable.

He'd spoken with Dr. Morrison at length and he'd told her about Layla and how things were going between them. He surprised himself with his revelations. It was the first time he'd taken what had been going on in his head and in his heart about Layla, turned them into words and said them out loud.

Dr. Morrison joked that it seemed that Layla was angling for her job, but she was very pleased that he'd found someone like her. She could sense the change in him and it was a good change, a positive one. And he grudgingly agreed that she was right about him coming to the Harbor.

He hadn't talked to Dr. Morrison about meeting his buddy's wife, Kim. It was an issue that he was still wrestling with. Who did he owe his allegiance to: the SEALs and the U.S. government or to his friends who gave up their lives under his watch? It was a question that ate away at him. What was the right thing to do? And now that Kim had actually confronted him…his wall of resistance weakened. He'd been trained to be bound by silence, even under the most inhumane conditions and physical torture. But there was no training that prepared him to look into the eyes of a woman who loved her husband and lie to her.

He started back toward the main building and walked into the lounge, hoping to spot Layla. Many of the tables were occupied, but he didn't see her. As he was about to leave, Lincoln approached him.

"Hey, how are you?" Lincoln greeted. "Lawson, right? Maurice?"

Maurice offered a short smile and a nod. "That's me."

"I try to put a name with the faces of my guests. Sometimes I do better than others," he joked. "Haven't seen you around too much. How are you enjoying your stay?"

"It's been great. Better than I expected to be honest. Accommodations, food, atmosphere…no complaints from me."

"That's a testimonial that we can use," he said with a grin. "Heading out?" he asked with a lift of his chin toward the exit.

"Yeah."

"I'll walk with you."

"How long have you been in business?" Maurice asked.

Lincoln pushed the door open and held it for Maurice. "Hmm, this will be seven years in August."

"I would think it would be kind of risky, seasonal, I guess I should say."

"True. But at the time that I opened The Port, all I wanted was a complete change. I didn't care too much about the highs and lows of the guest flow." He snorted a laugh. "Not the most astute businessman in the world."

Maurice snatched a look at him and grinned. "Seemed to have worked out for you, though."

Lincoln bobbed his head in agreement. "There's something special about this place…and of course my wife, Desiree, is really the one who transformed it *and* me. It was our idea when we first got together…then things got crazy…we broke up and I came here, started our dream without her. And then I really nearly lost her when her art studio in New York burned down…with her inside."

"Whoa. A fire?"

"Yeah. Turned out to be arson." He pushed out a breath, shook his head and chuckled lightly. "Fate is a funny thing, man. Of all the places that she could have gone to recover and get her head right, she wound up here—without even knowing I was running the place. But it didn't really come together until we did. Oh, let me clarify," he said, holding up his hand, "until she was ready. Women," he said with a chuckle.

They turned along the path and Lincoln acknowledged several of the guests that they passed.

"So, what do you do when you're not chilling on the beach and tossing back drinks?"

Maurice smirked. "I was in the Navy."

"Really. Wow. *Was?* Is that how you got hurt, if you don't mind me asking?"

"Yeah," he answered quietly.

"My uncle was in the military. Marines. Career soldier. Totally committed and dedicated. He got hurt in the Gulf War and couldn't go back." He slowly shook his head. "Really screwed with his head. He was never able to accept it and adjust to civilian life. And the fact that he was alone, no wife, no kids and refused to get help only made a bad situation worse."

"What eventually happened to him?"

Lincoln momentarily gripped Maurice's shoulder. "I don't need to lay all that on you, bro, get my uncle's story in your head." They kept walking. "You seem like you have it together."

Maurice sidestepped that comment. "How long have you been married?"

"Five years."

"What about you? Married, engaged, accounted for?"

Maurice chuckled and shook his head. "Naw, not

at the moment." He thought about Layla and if she would ever fill any of those parts of his life.

"As a matter of fact, we're having our anniversary party this weekend."

"Nice. Congratulations."

They continued along the path toward the guest cottages.

"You're more than welcome to come."

"Thanks, but I wouldn't want to impose."

"Please, no imposition. The more the merrier. Bring a guest if you want."

He glanced at Lincoln. "I'll think about it. How's that?"

"Good enough. Friday night. Eight o'clock." He dug a business card out of his pocket and handed it to Maurice. "If you decide to come, call me and I'll give you the details."

"Sure. Thanks." Maurice pocketed the card.

They came to the juncture in the path.

"I'm up that way," Maurice said raising his cane in the direction of his cottage.

"Cool." Lincoln stuck out his hand. "Nice to meet you."

They shook hands.

"Call me," Lincoln said and started to turn off down the path then stopped. "Hey, if you're into it, you should check out the spa. My wife's sorority sister runs the place. Everyone tells me she's amazing."

"Uh, yeah. I can vouch for that."

Lincoln studied him for a minute and a slow grin of unspoken understanding moved across his mouth. "Hope to see you Friday, man."

Maurice gave him a nod and headed toward his cottage but changed directions. He wanted to see Layla. Needed to, actually. He walked toward her cottage, hoping that she was there, only to find that she wasn't.

He stood on her porch for a moment, then took out his cell phone and punched in her number. The phone rang several times before going to her voice mail. He hesitated before leaving a message.

"Hi, it's Maurice. I was hoping we could have a late dinner or a nightcap, if you don't have plans. Call me."

He covered the two steps of the porch and began the walk back to his place when he looked down the path and saw Layla coming in his direction and an inexplicable wave of happiness moved through his limbs. He felt lifted. It was the only way he could explain it.

As he followed her approach, she was unaware that he watched her. She had her phone to her ear. There was a carefree air about her, an aura that was devoid of the clouds that often hovered over him. She seemed to carry a light within her that brightened everything in her path. It sounded crazy in his own head to even think along those lines, like some love struck poet, but that's what it felt like.

The curve in the path straightened and when she followed it she saw Maurice. Her step momentarily faltered as she cupped her eyes with her hand to shield them from the glare of the setting sun before she continued.

She stopped in front of him. "I just listened to your voice message about dinner tonight."

"I don't usually drop in on ladies unannounced, but I wanted to see you."

Her soft gaze moved slowly over his face, reacquainting herself with his handsome features and all the anxiety that she'd had about what she'd seen dissipated. "I'm glad you did. Want to come in for a minute?"

He reached out and tucked her hair behind her ear. "Believe me, baby, if I did we could forget about dinner."

Her face flooded with heat. She bit down on her lip. "Oh," she finally breathed. "Um, well, what time did you want to have dinner?"

"How's eight-thirty? Will that give you enough time? There's a late set jazz cruise. Showtime is ten. We can have dinner on the deck."

She beamed, feeling suddenly giddy inside. "Sounds great. I'll be ready."

Maurice stroked his thumb across her bottom lip and the pit of her belly fluttered in response. "See you then."

Layla bobbed her head, brushed by him, thrilling at the feel of his chest brushing against her bare arm, and went inside.

The corner of Maurice's mouth lifted ever so slightly. There *was* something special about this place and definitely something special about Layla Brooks. He started off toward his cottage. Maybe he *would* ask her about the party. But why hadn't she said anything to him about it?

Chapter 19

Layla was thrilled out of her mind when they boarded the ship and she discovered that Dexter Brown, protégée of Wynton Marsalis, was the headliner for the evening *and* that they had front row seats. It took all of her home training not to start squealing like a teen groupie and jumping up and down.

"You knew?" she cried, and squeezed Maurice's hard biceps.

He grinned. "Yeah. Thought you might like that." He helped her into her seat that faced the stage. He maneuvered his chair next to hers.

"And these seats…" She put her purse on the table. "How did you manage them?" She couldn't stop grinning.

"Dexter and I have played together at a few jam sessions overseas. He told me he was in town and got us the seats."

Her eyes widened. Her mouth opened, but she couldn't get the words to come out.

Maurice put his forefinger under her chin and gently pushed it up.

"You *know* Dexter Brown? You've played with him?" she finally stuttered.

He nodded slowly with an almost smug grin on his face.

She gave a quick shake of her head. "Wow. I mean, when you said you played, you were so low key about it. But you really play, play."

He shrugged his left shoulder.

"What else don't I know about you?"

He pursed his lips. His gaze drifted away for a moment then settled back on Layla's expectant expression. "There's a lot I want to tell you."

The rising sound of applause halted their conversation as Dexter took to the stage and opened with his classic hit "Come Sunrise."

Maurice reached over, took Layla's hand and brought it to his lips. He placed a featherlight kiss on her knuckles.

Layla's heart thumped and the dark, hungry look in his eyes set her blood on simmer. What this man could do to her with a simple look totally unnerved her.

A waitress stopped at their table and took their drink and dinner order.

Maurice bobbed his head to the music while he idly ran his thumb lazily across Layla's hand sending shivers through her with every caress. She shifted in her seat even as she wondered what he wanted to tell her.

Halfway through the set, Dexter addressed the enthusiastic audience. He thanked them for coming out and promised to play all of his hits, but he wanted to acknowledge a friend of his, a war veteran and an accomplished pianist.

Layla felt Maurice stiffen when Dexter called out his name and asked him to join him onstage.

Maurice waved his hand "no," and shook his head, but Dexter and the audience insisted.

"Go, go…" Layla urged. "Please." She squeezed his hand.

His gaze tightened and sucked her in. "For you," he murmured and a shiver ran up her spine. Maurice drew in a deep breath and slowly pushed himself up from his seat and joined Dexter and his band on the small stage. The piano player offered his seat.

"How about we do some Herbie Hancock?" Dexter said to the crowd who roared their approval. He looked to Maurice who nodded in agreement.

Maurice placed his fingers on the keys and smoothly launched into the iconic tune "'Round Midnight." Dexter supported the lilting melody, playing beneath and between the stylized piano notes.

Layla was transfixed, mesmerized not only by the beauty of the music but by the effortless skill that Maurice exuded. His eyes were closed at points as his fingers stroked the keys, teased them, caressed them, and bent them to his will. His hard body swayed like a leaf in a gentle breeze and his expression was one of total peace.

Too soon it came to an end and Layla was pulled from the almost dreamlike state to join in the thunderous applause.

Maurice took a short bow from the piano bench then slowly stood and was embraced in a strong hug and a slap on the back from Dexter before he returned to the table.

"That was…you were incredible," Layla said in awe.

His dark eyes sparkled and he couldn't hold back the smile that easily lit up the room.

"Thanks," he said softly.

"You can really play."

He chuckled and lowered his head. He reached for his glass of bourbon and took a refreshing swallow.

Layla leaned back in her seat, still beaming with the pride of knowing him and having experienced the magic of his playing. *Oh those magic fingers*.

Maurice and Layla couldn't keep a conversation going between them for the balance of the evening.

Everyone that passed their table for the rest of the night stopped by to congratulate him and ask if he had a CD that they could purchase. Maurice was gracious to them all as he accepted their accolades but disappointed them with no CD on the horizon.

By the time the evening came to an end, Layla felt as if she'd been on the red carpet up to and including the flash of cameras that took their picture with Dexter.

Layla was still grinning as they disembarked from the boat and out into the evening. She slipped her arm through Maurice's as they leisurely strolled back to Maurice's car that was parked near the end of the dock.

"What an incredible evening. Thank you," Layla said.

"Glad you enjoyed yourself."

She looked up at him and was drawn to the inviting smile on his lips. "Very much. Now I know what life would be like with a superstar," she teased.

He chuckled and hugged her close.

They walked slowly along the dock, enjoying the sultry breeze that blew in off the water and Layla suddenly realized that Maurice's limp was barely noticeable. He wasn't using his cane tonight either, and he appeared to be pain free. Inwardly she smiled but decided not to bring it up and draw attention to her observation. When his mind and spirit were cleared, whether it be through massage, making love and now she realized, through music, they compelled him to take his mind off of himself and allowed the pain to drift into the background.

"Early day for you tomorrow?" he asked when they stopped in front of his car. He opened her door.

"First client is at eleven."

His eyes crinkled with his smile. "Good."

Layla slid onto the delicious leather seat and Maurice shut the door behind her.

Maurice settled in the car, turned on the ignition and eased the car onto the road for the drive back.

"I ran into Lincoln Davenport earlier today."

"Desi's husband..."

"Yeah, real cool guy. We talked for a while. Actually he invited me to their anniversary party this weekend."

Layla turned halfway in her seat. "You're kidding. I'd planned to ask you to go with me."

Maurice took a quick glance at her. "Were you really going to ask me to go?"

The atmosphere suddenly shifted. "Ye-ss," she stammered. "Why would you think that I wouldn't ask you?" Her earlier doubts leapt to the forefront.

His jaw flexed. "From what I gather, these are longtime friends of yours, almost like family. I figured it was that kind of thing. But Lincoln insisted that wasn't the case." He made the turn out of the center of town and took the road toward The Port. "Since you never mentioned it..."

"I'd planned to...wanted to..."

"Look, it's not a big deal. Forget it. Not that serious." He reached for the dial on the CD player and within moments they were awash in Luther Vandross's "A House is Not a Home."

Layla stared out the front window, with her fingers knotted together on her lap. In a nanosecond the vibe had changed from hot to glacial. She wasn't sure what had just happened.

The Port was visible up ahead and within moments they would be pulling up in front of her place. And then what?

"Maurice..."

"Hmmm?"

"I held off asking you to the party because to be honest from one day to the next I'm never sure what's going on with us."

She watched his profile harden in stages as if it was being cast in cement.

He made the turn onto the property. Her heart raced and her body grew warm with anxiety. They drove pass the main building toward the cottages. Hers was to the right but Maurice made the left at the junction in the road. She pressed her lips together to keep from asking him where he was going.

He continued beyond the spread of cottages until he reached the edge of the property that opened onto the beach. He turned the car off and rested his wrists along the steering wheel.

Layla ran her tongue across her bottom lip and waited—for what she wasn't sure.

Maurice turned halfway in his seat to face her. "You're right."

"Right?"

"Yeah, about the direction that this relationship is going." He ran his hand along his chin. "Look, in another couple of weeks I'll be back in Brooklyn and you'll be doing what you do." He lowered his head for a moment.

The muscles in her throat constricted. She blinked away the burn in her eyes.

"The thing is…it's not what I want."

Layla's stomach clenched. Her gaze jumped to his. What was he saying?

"But I still got a lot of shit to work out, Layla. And I'm not going to be somebody's rebound either—on top of everything else." He pushed out a breath then reached over and threaded a strand of hair behind her ear. "You're good for me. I know that. But I gotta be good for myself first."

Layla clasped his hand and held it to her cheek. "Do you want to try?" she asked on a whisper and a prayer.

"Let's see how the next few weeks go," he offered.

"And then what?"

"We'll see if we want to make something happen."

She considered what he said. It did make sense. Their relationship, as it stood, was always on a short fuse. It made things exciting and unpredictable but also uncertain in a way that had her wanting to run in the opposite direction to keep from getting hurt again. He was right. He was still in the healing stage on several levels and she did need to make sure that Maurice was what she wanted and not simply someone to fill a void.

Layla released a long, slow breath then nodded her head in agreement. "All right," she finally whispered.

The tightness around his dark eyes eased when the storm cloud of his sleek brows settled back in place. He leaned across the gearbox until he was out of focus and his lips tenderly met hers.

Her heart rose to her throat as heat moved through her veins. Maurice threaded his fingers through the back of her hair and eased her into the kiss. The fullness of his mouth coaxed hers open to accept the exploration of his tongue that was so sweet and tinged with a heady hint of bourbon.

Layla sighed softly. Her head spun from the pounding of her pulse. She would give in willingly to Maurice. She knew that deep in her soul. He was a complex, maze of a man. Every time she thought she understood him, he shifted and revealed yet another part of himself while at the same time remaining inaccessible. It was a maddening and thrilling roller-coaster ride of emotions. She didn't want the ride to stop.

Maurice eased back and she felt as if she'd been

cast out to sea—adrift. Her eyes fluttered open and searched his face.

"Your place or mine?" he asked. The deep timbre of his voice vibrated down to her toes.

"You're asking me?" she teased.

"This time." A sensuous grin curved his mouth.

"Yours."

He put the car in gear. "I'm as good at taking orders as giving them," he said, turning the car in the direction of his cottage.

Chapter 20

"Like some wine?" Maurice asked, once they were inside his place.

"Sure." Layla strolled to the center of the living space and sat down on the padded stool at the granite-topped island.

Maurice took down two glasses from the overhead cupboard and retrieved the bottle of white wine from the wine cooler below the counter. He filled their glasses halfway and sat opposite her.

Layla studied his every moment. Even with the slight stiffness from his injury, his movements were controlled, sleek and clad all in black, darkly dangerous. She could almost see his stealthlike maneuvers in the mountains and jungles, zeroing in on his objective, or leading his team into enemy territory, barking orders and charging forward, armed and strapped. The images gave her a rush.

He raised his glass, which eased her from her daydream.

"To a great night."

Layla tapped her glass lightly against his. She crossed her legs to quell the drumbeat between her thighs.

Maurice studied her over the rim of his glass before setting it down.

"I'll be heading back to the city in about two weeks."

"Oh." She sipped her wine and savored it in her mouth before swallowing.

"Right after the Fourth."

"Work I guess?" It was both a statement and a question.

"Gotta make a living." He finished off his wine. "Shrink bills," he tapped his temple, "therapy," he rubbed his leg. "Co-pay."

"Tell me about your father," she said out of the blue, taking them both by surprise.

The muscles in his cheeks tightened. "My father?" He snorted a laugh. "Why?"

She shrugged slightly. "It'll tell me more about you, the boy you were, the man you became."

He blew out air through his nostrils and reached

for the wine bottle. He refilled his glass and topped off hers. "You sound like my shrink."

"I don't mean to."

"Well, you do." He pushed up from his seat and walked over to the French doors that led to the back deck.

"I want to know you better."

"And asking about my father is going to do that for you?" He kept his back to her.

"Maybe," she said softly.

His broad shoulders resembled solid rock encased in soft black cotton. Layla wanted to touch him, bring him back to her, work the tightness out of his neck and the curve of his spine. She felt him slipping away. That was not her intent. She started to get up and go to him, but his distant voice held her in place.

"He was a hard man," he said. His voice came from a long ago place.

She watched his shoulders slowly rise and settle.

"When I think about him...I try to remember a time when he wasn't demanding something of me. If it wasn't school, it was sports, friends, jobs, how I dressed. Hammering, hammering." He pounded his fist into his palm. "I spent most of my life trying to please him and live up to the impossible expectations that he had."

She wanted to ask him about his mother and

where she fit into his life but dared not interrupt him now that he was finally talking.

"My mother…" he began as if reading her mind, "she left when I was around ten. What mother leaves her child?" He briefly glanced at her over his shoulder, his dark eyes reflecting the deep, unforgotten wounds. His jaw clenched and he turned away again. He slung his hands into his pockets, his dark silhouette illuminated by the light from the moon over the water. "A part of me thought that if I didn't please him, he would leave like my mother did."

Layla's heart clenched. She could barely imagine what he must have gone through. She bit down on her bottom lip.

"Stupid, huh? But that's how kids think."

She got up from the stool and slowly crossed the space to stand behind him. She slid her arms around his waist and rested her head against his back. "I'm sorry," she whispered.

He clasped her hands with one of his. "Don't be. It was a long time ago. I'm over it."

But he wasn't. She could tell by the words he chose to use and how he lived his life. Of all the professions to select he decided to become a Navy SEAL, one of the most dangerous, challenging, grueling professions on the planet, cloaked in secrecy and code words. He chose a profession that didn't leave room for error, one that demanded the ultimate best from its members. Yet, on the other hand

he was a gifted pianist, a skill that left all kinds of
room for improvisation and change—one part of his
life juxtaposed against the other in constant conflict.
She shut her eyes.

"I graduated nearly two years early, top of my
class, went to his alma mater, studied finance and
even landed a job on Wall Street, never took it
though, much to my father's fury." He shook his
head. "Never saw him so pissed off." He drew in a
long breath. "Moved out right after that. Bounced
around, played with a few bands…met Dexter." She
felt his smile. "My father called me…while I was in
Paris…he was upset…said everything was coming
apart…and the only one who could help him was my
uncle Branford. He wasn't making any sense and the
connection was crap. We got cut off. Next time I saw
my father was at his funeral."

For a moment the air stopped moving. She could
feel his pulse pounding through his veins. She
pressed her head tighter against his back willing
her mind and body to absorb his hurt and replace it
with healing energy.

Layla came around to stand in front of him. She
looked up into his eyes and then cupped his face in
her hands and rose up to kiss him.

He drew her to him, held her as if he would never
let her go. His mouth moved hungrily over hers with
an urgency that stole her breath away.

His fingertips pressed into her flesh as a low groan rose up from his throat.

She held on, certain that she would fall from a great height if she ever let him go. Heat unfurled deep in her belly and rushed to her head, banged in her veins.

His mouth dropped to her exposed neck where he planted hot kisses, laved her with his tongue to send jolts of electricity shimmering through her.

"I want you," he groaned, hot and heavy in her ear. His thumbs brushed the underside of her breasts then glided upward to caress them.

Layla whimpered in delight. It was so hot. So hot. She wanted to tear her clothes from her body to gain some relief.

Maurice shifted and his hands were under her dress, hiking it up above her hips. He hooked his fingers along the elastic band of her panties and pulled them down. And then he was on his knees, between her legs with his mouth pressed against her sex.

Her legs trembled, but he held her tightly by her hips. His tongue slid along her clit and found her wet and ready.

Tenderly he suckled the hardened bud until she was a mass of electrified sensation.

Her fingers dug into his shoulders. Her head was flung back as the intensity rose higher and higher. She was certain she was screaming with pleasure as he delved deeper, faster, teasing her in that deliciously sinful way of his.

She was on the brink of coming. Her breath came in short, hot gasps. Every sinew in her body was on fire. Her muscles tightened and then trembled uncontrollably as the mind-numbing climax slammed into her.

She cried out his name over and over as wave after wave of release washed through her leaving her limp and totally satisfied.

She realized that Maurice was standing in front of her. The room seemed out of focus. Her heart was still racing. She felt her knees give way, but Maurice had his arm around her waist. His hand slid between her thighs and he pushed a finger inside her. Instinctively her insides clenched around his finger and she trembled.

"We're not finished," he said urgently. He took her by the hand led her into his bedroom. Quickly he rid her of her clothing and then his.

Maurice pulled her onto the bed. The lay facing each other. He ran his hand languidly along her side, down the dip in her waist, over the curve of her hip, before dipping his head to suck a needy nipple into his mouth.

"Ohhh…."

He nipped her just a little with his teeth and her hips pushed up against him.

Maurice groaned. His erection throbbed. He

stretched toward the end table and dug around inside for a condom. He turned onto his back, put the packet between his teeth and tore it open. Skillfully he rolled on the thin sheath.

He turned to Layla. She moved toward him and eagerly gave him the kiss that he sought and then his hands, his mouth, his tongue were everywhere at once, igniting every nerve in her body. And then she was pinned beneath him, her legs spread wide on either side of him.

He stroked her thighs, coaxed her knees until they bent and then he was inside her and all the air stuck in her lungs.

Tiny explosions of light went off behind her lids as the length and breadth of him filled her.

He remained perfectly still, relishing the exquisite sensation of her wet, velvet heat that wrapped around him like a glove.

Layla tried to raise her hips, to heighten the friction, to feel more of him, but he held her perfectly still.

He used his weight to hold down her hips while he pulled slowly out of her and then back in with the same erotic deliberateness.

Layla whimpered.

"Sssh." He pushed into her again and again then covered her mouth with his to swallow her cries. "Spread your legs for me," he whispered against her mouth. He nuzzled her neck. She did as he asked. He thrust deeper, held them there then pulled out slowly until only the swollen tip remained inside her.

She tried to rise up, to get him back, but he held her fast.

"Not yet. Just give in to the experience. Feel it. Feel me. Feel me," he groaned and began to move, slow and steady, in and out, each time hitting a new spot, igniting another delicious sensation.

Every fiber of her being tingled and throbbed and pulsed. Her thoughts swam. She was a ball of unbelievable feeling, transported out of her body.

She gripped the sheets in her fists to keep from screaming as the first burst of her climax roared through her.

Maurice groaned as her insides gripped him in a vice. He pushed her thighs apart, flexed his hips and rammed into her over and over as the world exploded into a million lights and doused them in their flame.

Layla curled in Maurice's arms. Her thoughts were cloudy, her body still hummed. Her limbs felt leaden. She was sure she wouldn't be able to move for days. He stroked her hair.

"You okay?" he asked quietly.

"Hmmm."

He kissed the top of her head then pulled the sheet up over them. "Get some sleep."

"Will you go with me to the party?" she mumbled.

"I'll think about it. Sleep. You have to work to-morrow. I don't." He kissed her again and she acquiesced into a peaceful deep sleep.

Chapter 21

"Morning."

Layla's eyes fluttered open. Maurice gradually came into focus, standing above her holding a steaming cup of coffee. He was shirtless. His pajama pants hung low on his slender hips.

A smile eased across her mouth. "Morning." Her tongue felt thick. She reached for the cup. "Thank you."

He sat down on the side of the bed. "Sleep okay?"

She nodded. "You?"

"Like a well-fed baby." He grinned. "It's almost ten."

She pushed her hair away from her face and covered a yawn. "Do you always get up so early after... a long night?" Her cheeks heated.

"Years of training." His eyes crinkled. "I've been up since six."

She blinked back her surprise. "Wow, I feel like a real slacker." She sipped more coffee and started to feel a little more alert. She set the cup down on the nightstand and sat up against the pillows. She pulled her knees toward her chest and felt the ache. A flash from the night before teased her thoughts.

"Want me to run you a shower or you want to do that at your place?"

"My place. But thanks for the offer." She took him in. "How's the leg."

As if thinking about it for the first time, he reached down and massaged his thigh.

"Better than it's been in a very long time." His eyes moved over her face. "I owe that to you."

"I wish I could take the credit for that but I can't. You have to do the work." She tossed the sheet aside and stood.

"Hmm. You look very edible in the morning, Ms. Brooks."

She snatched the sheet from the bed and wrapped it around her naked body then padded off to the bathroom.

They stood framed in his doorway.

"See you later?" he asked.

"I'd like that."

"I'll stop by the spa around three."

"Okay." She pressed her fingers to her lips and

then placed them against his stubbled cheek. "See you later."

Layla sailed through her morning and gave extra special attention to each of her clients. All of them gushed about how good she was, how wonderful they felt and that they were going to recommend her to all of their friends.

At three on the dot, Maurice showed up. She locked the door and devoted the next hour and a half to making him forget everything that wasn't her.

For the rest of the week they spent all of their free time together, talking, laughing, exploring the town, strolling along the beach, waking up together in the morning and sleeping together at night.

When she wasn't with him she felt as if a part of her was missing, and she counted down the hours until she would see him again.

Maurice was actually happy. He felt good inside and out. The pain was virtually gone. The nightmares had vanished. The thoughts that constantly twisted inside him were pushed to a corner of his mind, no longer dominating everything that he did or how he felt.

He was only slightly reluctant to conclude that it was because Layla was in his life. She had opened up a space in his soul and entered it. They'd known each other for almost two months but he felt as if he'd been waiting all his life for her. The fear of his growing feelings for Layla was still there but he wanted to battle them and win.

He'd opted for a crisp white shirt beneath the midnight blue suit that Layla had helped him pick out on one of their excursions into town. He grinned at his reflection in the mirror. She had great taste. He slid his tie around his neck.

Although he'd been initially reluctant to attend the party, he'd rather do the mix and mingle thing than spend an evening apart from Layla and run the risk of the single men ogling his woman.

His thoughts jerked to a halt. His fingers stilled. *His woman?* Wow, when had that notion slipped in and found a home? Was Layla his woman or was this thing that they had going on a passing fling—a result of the magic of The Port?

He straightened his tie, took his wallet from the dresser and put it in his pocket.

Whatever it was, it was changing him in ways that he had never expected. Would it last? Was it real? By habit he massaged his thigh. He looked toward his cane that stood propped in the corner. Not tonight. Tonight he would be like every other man.

Layla stepped into her killer heels that were definitely designed for style and not longevity on the dance floor. She did a pirouette in the mirror and the skirt of her knee-length, teal-colored cocktail dress fanned out around her long legs. The halter top aptly supported the weight of her breasts and the deep opened back teased the imagination.

She dabbed her favorite scent behind her ears, the pulse points at her wrists and in the valley of her breasts. A final coat of tinted lip gloss and she was ready for her night out with Maurice.

As excited as she was about the event itself, she was equally apprehensive. For the most part she and Maurice had created their own cocoon, a fantasy world of sorts. It was only the two of them. This would be the first time that they were together in a big social setting, among her friends.

In the time that she'd gotten to know Maurice she knew that his mood could shift at the drop of a hat. He could go from open and gregarious to dark and dangerously distant in the blink of an eye, and she was never sure what would set him off. She knew that most of it was a result of the demons that he still wrestled with and the issues that remained off-topic, and the flare up of pain that was a constant reminder that he was no longer the man that he once was and could never return to the life that he believed defined him.

Her fingers shook ever so slightly as she slipped her earrings in her lobes. It was more than that. She should have told him about tonight. Desiree told her as much as well. But things had been going so well between them and she didn't want anything to upset the balance that they'd established.

She drew in a breath and faced her reflection. It will all work out, she inwardly chanted.

Her stomach tightened at the sound of the knock on her front door. She prayed she'd done the right thing.

Maurice's eyes lit up the dark when he saw her standing in the doorway.

"You look…incredible."

"Thank you," she managed unable to take her eyes off of her chocolate candy in front of her. "And you…"

He grinned. "You have good taste. Ready?"

She nodded. She took her tiny purse from the table by the door and they headed out.

When they drove up to Melanie's home, the entire landscape and two-story house was awash in muted white lights. The soft strains of music drifted to them on the balmy breeze. The air was filled with electric energy. Valets scurried about parking cars along the property and the well-heeled guests dotted the landscape in varying degrees of finery.

Maurice turned the keys over to the valet and Layla grabbed his hand. "I'm happy you decided to come."

He leaned down and gave her a quick kiss before they started along the path to the front door.

As usual, Melanie had outdone herself. The ground floor had been turned into a full dance area. All of the furniture had been removed. A four-piece band was set up near the back wall. Five massive linen-topped tables were lined from end to end with an assortment of cold and hot foods and everything from caviar to grilled salmon, roasted duck, steamed vegetables, and everything in between. And of course there was the dessert table that redefined decadent.

The bar took up another wall and servers in black and white outfits carried plates of tiny appetizers. It was all a little overwhelming to anyone who was unaccustomed to Melanie's extravagance. Layla grew up in this environment. And although she'd distanced herself from it in later years, it was still "just another party."

Layla felt Maurice tense next to her as they moved through the gathering guests. She gave his hand a reassuring squeeze and looked up to find his expression stiff and unyielding. His brows were drawn together in a tight line.

"I thought this was close friends," he said, looking around disparagingly. Images of Lawson family shindigs flashed in his head. All the pomp and circumstance and phony friendships, and purposeless conversations curled his stomach. A shaft of pain seized his leg.

"It is…sort of," she said, forcing cheer into her voice, hoping to ease the tension.

His jaw clenched.

She pressed her head against his arm. "Come on,

we're here to celebrate Desi and Lincoln's anniversary," she gently coaxed. "They're really cool people and so are their friends. We'll have fun. You'll see."

Maurice pushed out a breath of reluctant acceptance. "What's back there," he asked, lifting his chin in the direction of the yard.

"Let's go see." She took his hand to lead him out back just as Melanie and Claude approached.

"There you two are." Melanie hurried over to the couple and embraced Layla in a tight hug. "He's edible," she whispered in Layla's ear then stepped back.

"Mel, Claude, this is Maurice Lawson."

Maurice extended his hand to Melanie and then Claude. "Thanks for having me."

"Of course. Layla hasn't stopped talking about you. I've been dying to meet you."

A waitress approached with a tray of drinks. Melanie plucked a flute of champagne from the tray and the trio followed suit.

"To a wonderful evening," Claude said.

They touched glasses.

"Where are the guests of honor?" Layla asked.

"Out back. Come. I'll introduce you around." Melanie linked her arm through Layla's and the men walked behind them.

"Did you tell him?" Melanie whispered.

"No."

Melanie shot her a look of alarm. "I hope you know what you're doing."

"So do I," she said on a breath of hope.

They stepped through the opened French doors and out into a wonderland. Lights draped the trees, giving the night a starlike quality. The manicured lawn was covered in enormous white tents with circular tables beneath, all set with white china, sparkling silver and crystal glasses.

There was another band set up along the perimeter and a row of chafing tables with even more food. At least a hundred people floated around.

"There they are," Melanie said, pointing out Desiree and Lincoln across the lawn.

They wound their way around the tents to the guests of honor.

Desiree squealed in delight when she saw Layla. "So glad you're here," she said, squeezing her hands. She looked over to Maurice.

"So glad to officially meet you. We've been ships in the night for weeks." She grabbed Lincoln's arm. "Lincoln told me you two already met."

"Yes, we did." He smiled at Lincoln and they shook hands. "Good to see you."

"Yes, you too. Glad you decided to come. Have you all eaten?"

"No, we just got here."

"Well, there's plenty of everything," Melanie said. "Relax, eat, enjoy, mingle. I'm going to do my hostess thing." She tiptoed and pecked her husband's lips then wiped away the smudge of lipstick with the pad of her thumb before she flitted away.

"I don't know about you guys, but I could use a real drink," Claude said, holding up the delicate flute of champagne and making a face.

"Now you're talking," Lincoln agreed. "You game?" he asked Maurice.

"Sure, why not."

"In that case, if you ladies will excuse us," Claude said with a short bow. The three men walked off to the main house.

"Girl, I can see why your head is spinning over that man," Desiree said once the men were out of earshot.

Layla blushed and heaved a sigh. "Yeah, he's a special guy. I'm really falling for him, Desi, but..."

"But what?"

She lowered her head. "He's a hard man to get to know. There are layers to him that he won't uncover. Under all that virile exterior he has a lot of anger and guilt."

"About what?"

"His family for one."

"Ohh...and you didn't tell him, I take it."

She shook her head. "I know I should have said something but I'm hoping for the best."

"Listen," she placed her hand on Layla's arm. "One of the biggest mistakes I made was not being honest with Lincoln. It nearly destroyed our relationship. You know what we went through. If you want this man in your life then both of you have to be open with each other no matter how ugly it is. And I think it has to start with you. From what you tell me he's holding on to a lot of stuff. He's going to take his cues from you."

"You're right. I know that." She looked around. "I better go find him."

Claude was rounding up the tour, introducing Maurice to some of the guests along the way, and the guys wound up in his den where Claude pulled out his aged bottle of bourbon. He took out glasses from the bar and handed them out.

"So, what do you do?" Maurice asked as he glanced around the very masculine space of dark wood and inlaid cabinets.

"Oh, I thought you knew."

"Knew?"

"Yeah, I'm chief of staff for your uncle."

Maurice turned toward him. "My uncle…Branford?"

Claude smiled. "Yeah. Small world, huh? He's supposed to be coming tonight if he can get away."

Claude poured each tumbler half full. He raised his glass. "To my man Linc and five more years of marital bliss."

Maurice barely registered anything else. His thoughts raced in a dozen directions. Branford. Here. Did Layla know and if she did why didn't she say anything? She had to know that Claude worked for his uncle. Melanie was her god-sister. Anger simmered low in his gut. He tossed back his drink. The burn did nothing but stoke the fire inside.

The voices of Claude and Lincoln swirled around him. He'd spent the past ten years of his life staying away from the man that had ruined everything. He'd cut himself off from the family that stood by the man who'd had a hand in his own brother's suicide. The press ignored it. Friends told him to move on. And when he finally allowed someone to get close to him again, she betrayed him. Set him up.

The glass snapped in his hand.

"Whoa, hey, you all right?" Claude grabbed a towel from the bar and hurried over to Maurice.

He stared at his bleeding hand.

"What the...?" Lincoln sputtered, seeing the glass and blood.

Maurice took the towel and dabbed at his hand. "Guess I don't know my own strength."

"You need to get that looked at." Claude took the towel.

Maurice shook his head. "It's all right." He walked over to the sink and ran the water. He held his hand under the stream and gritted his teeth against the sting. "Not bad. Minor cut. Nothing serious." There was a small gash in his hand.

"Only see that on television," Lincoln tried to joke. He came up behind Maurice and put his hand on his back while Claude picked up glass off the floor and dumped it into the towel. "You good, man?" Linc asked quietly.

"Yeah. Thanks." He turned off the water.

Claude crossed the room toward the door. "We have a first-aid kit upstairs. I'll be right back," Claude said then came up short.

"So, here you are."

"Rafe." Claude went to the door and gave him a one arm bear hug. "Glad you made it, brother."

Several years earlier there had been a testosterone battle for Melanie's attention between Claude and Rafe. Rafe, as usual, was more interested in the possibility than the reality and never fully pursued her, bowing out gracefully to make room for Claude. In the ensuing years they'd developed a grudging admiration for the other.

"Yeah, yeah, you know I couldn't miss one of Melanie's parties, especially for my man Linc. Full house, as usual, I see." He glanced down at the blood-tinged towel in Claude's hand. "Accident?"

"Little something. I was going for the first-aid kit. Linc's inside," he said, tipping his head toward the interior of the den. "And your cousin, Maurice." He patted Rafe's shoulder. "Be back in a minute."

Rafe stepped fully into the den as Maurice turned from the sink.

Chapter 22

Layla looked over heads and in between bodies, hoping to spot Maurice. Maneuvering from one end of the house to the other was made more difficult by the guests that had doubled in size since her arrival. She was stopped several times by some of her clients who were in attendance and wanted to introduce her to others. She remained gracious, making quick small talk and promising to chat more later.

Just as she was about to go downstairs she ran into Claude.

"Claude, where is Maurice?"

"Down in the den. Had a little accident." He held up the gauze and surgical tape.

"Accident?" Her pulsed kicked up a notch. "What are you talking about?"

"Brother doesn't know his own strength. Broke a glass in his hand."

"What!"

"Relax, he's fine. Little flesh wound."

There was a flurry of activity that drew their attention to the main entrance.

The six foot four Senator Branford Lawson stood out like a beacon and with the charisma inherent in all good politicians the room gravitated toward him. He was *GQ* sharp in an obviously expensive steel gray suit, silver shirt and tie. His megawatt smile and smooth Southern charm lit up the room like the Fourth of July.

Layla felt light-headed. She had to find Maurice before he ran into his uncle. She grabbed the gauze and tape from Claude. "I can take it to him. Go greet your guest." She hurried off before he could protest.

Quickly she darted down the long hallway and around a corner to a mid-lower level and turned right. She heard raised voices and her heart jumped to her throat. She ran toward the den.

Lincoln was standing between Maurice and Rafe, doing his best to keep them from going at each other.

Maurice's face was a ball of fury. Veins stood out in his forehead and it looked as if his chest had expanded in size.

"You checked out!" Rafe shouted. "You never bothered to find out the truth."

"The truth! What fucking truth, the one my uncle made everyone believe?"

"Maurice!"

Three pairs of eyes turned toward the door. The look that Maurice threw at her rooted her to the spot. Pure, unadulterated rage poured from him. But what was worse than his anger was the look of betrayal that swam in his eyes. And it was directed at her.

Maurice pushed pass Lincoln and Rafe. "Stay away from me," he growled, pointing at Rafe with a warning finger. He stopped at the door.

Layla's heart thundered in her chest. She looked at him with pleading eyes.

"And you, too." He brushed by her and stormed out.

"Maurice…"

"Let him go. Give him time to cool off," Lincoln said, coming to her side.

Layla looked from one to the other. "What happened?"

Rafe adjusted his tie, almost a mirror image of his father in his younger years. Tall, sleek, wickedly handsome, and oozing with sexual charm. She hadn't seen Rafe in quite some time. He hadn't changed. If anything he was even more handsome.

"Layla, long time," he said in that smooth, easy lilt. "I take it you've met my long-lost cousin." He turned toward the bar and poured himself a drink. "You could do better, cher." He tossed the drink back and turned dark, brooding eyes on her.

Maurice strode through the house, blinded by his own rage. But the feeling of betrayal by the one person he'd allowed into his life had him by the throat. It burned his insides like acid. All he wanted to do was get as far away as he could from Layla, this place and the Lawsons.

Pain suddenly ripped through his thigh nearly bringing him to his knees as pushed past the guests to get outside and to his car. He grabbed the wall to steady himself, gritting his teeth in agony.

He drew in a long, shaky breath and started off again, his limp growing more pronounced with every step. The front door seemed miles away. Sweat broke out on his forehead. His stomach swam.

"Maurice?"

Through the haze of pain the image of his uncle came into focus in front of him.

Branford reached for him. "Are you all right, son?"

"Don't you touch me," he said through gritted teeth.

"Maurice, please, let me help you."

"Get away from me!" He forced one foot in front of the other and made his way out, followed by whispers and wide-eyed curiosity.

It seemed like an eternity before the valet brought

his car around. Through the searing pain he finally managed to get behind the wheel and pull off. He felt like he might black out and had to take deep breaths to keep his head clear. He held the wheel in a death grip as he wound along the dark, winding road back to The Port.

Mercifully, he arrived in front of his cottage without incident. He needed to get his medication. He opened the car door but the pain was so bad he couldn't move his leg to get out.

Images of the Black Hawk going down into the mountains, the scream of the engine, the flashing indicator lights, the rush of adrenaline as the team prepared for the crash and then impact and the heat, raced through his mind. He'd been thrown clear of the fiery crash with a hunk of hot metal embedded in his leg. But he didn't feel it. All he could think about was getting to his buddies, trying to find them in the black smoke and flames. He couldn't walk, so he crawled. He dragged the two survivors to safety before he'd blacked out. He used that same inner strength to pull himself out of the car and drag himself into the house.

The party continued. The band played. The food was consumed and the drinks washed it all down. They danced. They laughed. They partied the night away.

Melanie and Claude took center stage toward the

close of the evening to thank their guests for helping them to bring in the summer season and to celebrate the five-year anniversary of her dear friends Desiree and Lincoln Davenport.

Holding hands and beaming, Desiree and Lincoln joined Melanie and Claude and thanked their gracious hosts and everyone who joined them for their special day.

Layla stood on the sidelines, numb. How could she have been so arrogant as to think she could fix things? She of all people knew the depths of Maurice's rift with his family. It was a part of his life that he kept buried so deep that he wouldn't talk about it, other than he held his uncle responsible for his father's suicide. Why or how he would never say.

Stupidly she thought if they could see each other they could find a way to open the lines of communication. She knew that there was a part of Maurice that ached for the family that he'd lost. Even though his relationship with his father was fraught with issues, David Lawson was still his father and when he lost that figure of authority, he filled that void with the Navy. Now that the Navy was no longer a part of his life, he was emotionally adrift. So, what better anchor than your family, the people who should be there for you when you were in need? She believed that. But she was wrong.

She should have listened to Mel and Desi when they told her to tell him that Rafe and Branford may attend the party. But she knew that if she did, Maurice would never have come. That outcome certainly would not have been worse than what happened tonight.

She needed to go to him and try to explain, get him to understand that she'd never intended to deceive him. No matter what happened after tonight, she couldn't let him go back home believing that.

"Hey."

The low, soothing voice floated to her. Layla blinked, bringing the room back into focus. Rafe was standing in front of her.

She straightened, forced a smile. "Rafe."

He tilted his head to the side and observed her from beneath silken lashes. "You look like you could use a drink."

She leaned against the wall and folded her arms. "I'm fine. Thanks."

"Are you now?"

She lifted her chin. "Yes, I am."

He smirked. "How long have you known my very angry cousin?"

The swift shift in conversation threw her for a moment. She ran her tongue across her lips. "Awhile."

"So, I guess you know the story."

Her gaze snapped to his. He was staring. It unnerved her. Rafe had a way of looking at a woman as if she was a delicacy.

"The story?"

"The great scandal," he said in a mocking tone. He sipped his drink. His eyes roved over her. Her pulse quickened.

"I know a little," she said. "He blames your father for his father's death."

The corner of his lush mouth quirked in a half grin. "Hmmm. So, it would seem."

"What's that supposed to mean?"

His right brow rose every so slightly. "That there are always two sides to a story." He finished off his drink and deposited it on the tray of a passing waiter.

"And you know both sides," she challenged.

"No, I don't," he said surprising her. "I don't much cotton to my old man and how he lives his life. He doesn't much care for how I live mine either. I guess you could say we have a strained relationship," he continued in that lullaby voice of his. "My father may be a lot of things, but he's not a liar." He grinned. "Probably the only decent thing I can say about him."

"Even though you don't know what happened, you still believe your father?"

"Yes, cher, I do. And I never say 'I do,' lightly." He smiled.

"Why should I believe you?"

"Because the one trait that I get from my beyond reproach father is that I don't lie either," he said, the last word soft as a song. "Especially to ladies in distress."

"I'm not in distress," she said petulantly.

"Of course you are. The man you care deeply about walked out on you and you want to make it right somehow. There's nothing wrong with that. It's a shame that my stubborn cousin doesn't see what an ass he's being."

Layla stiffened.

"We were close once."

There was that shift again. Maurice did the same thing. Must run in the family. Her eyes cut to his face. He was looking away.

"Best friends growing up. I was the only one that he talked to about how things were at home and how different it was for him when he came to stay with us during school breaks. His father rode him endlessly. Nothing was ever good enough for Uncle David, but Maurice…" he slowly shook his head, "he loved his father." He pursed his mouth in thought. "That's where he and I were always different. He kept trying to please Uncle David. Me, I didn't care what my father wanted. I lived for the battle." He chuckled lightly. "Still do." His dark eyes settled on Layla.

"What happened between you two?"

"After Uncle David…we drifted apart. He cut himself off from all of us. When he first went into the Navy, he'd send me a card from time to time and then it stopped." He slid his hand into his pants pocket and braced his shoulder against the wall.

"Layla, there you are." Melanie approached them.

She slid her arm around Rafe's waist. "Don't let this man dazzle you with his charm."

"You wound me, cher." He gave her a devilish grin.

"Why don't you stay here tonight, Layla? Everyone is starting to leave. We can chat and unwind," she offered, allowing Layla to read between the lines.

"I'm fine, sis. I'm going to head back."

"Did you drive?" Rafe asked.

"I…" She'd come with Maurice. "No."

"I'll drive you. Staying in town?"

"No. At The Port."

"Whenever you're ready."

"Are you sure it's no trouble?

"Tending to a lady is never any trouble."

"Oh, Rafe…you are so awful," Melanie teased. "Be sure to leave him at the front door," she playfully warned, then leaned up and kissed his cheek. "Behave yourself and don't stay away so long." She turned to Layla. "We'll talk tomorrow." She gave her a brief hug and swished away.

Rafe watched her departure with appreciation. He turned back to Layla. "Ready?"

"Yes, but let me say good-night to Desiree and Lincoln."

"I'll get the car brought up front and meet you outside."

"Thanks. I won't be long."

When Rafe walked toward the front entrance he

spotted his father seated with Claude deep in conversation. He walked over. They glanced up when he stopped in front of them.

"I'm going to drive Layla back to The Port then head to my hotel in town."

"Did you speak with Maurice?"

If Rafe didn't know better, he'd swear that his father actually looked hurt.

"I wouldn't call what we did having a conversation if that's what you want to know."

"What the hell happened, Rafe? What did you say to him?"

Rafe snorted a laugh. "What did *I* say? Like there was something that I could have possibly said to make him act any different than he's been acting for the past ten years?" He threw his hands up in the air in faux exasperation. "I have no damn clue. Maybe if you tell him what he's been asking you, what we've all been asking you for the past decade we wouldn't be having this conversation." He glared at his father who slowly and deliberately rose to his full height. "Before he winds up like Uncle David."

Branford visibly blanched. The two men faced each other in a silent standoff. Branford threw his son one last hard look before turning and walking away.

Rafe stood there for a moment. He lowered his head, pulled himself together and said good-night to Claude.

He stepped out into the cooling night and gazed up at the blanket of stars. Some things never changed. He gave the valet his ticket and waited for his car and Layla.

Chapter 23

Layla and Rafe talked quietly in the cocoon of his car for more than an hour. He was nothing like the cavalier man he often presented himself to be. Charming, yes, but introspective as well, surprising her with his openness.

"It was hard losing Maurice as a friend," he was saying. "We both had fathers that wanted us to be like them. So, we understood each other in a way that my sisters and my brother never did. We'd always been there for each other. I wanted to be there for him when he lost his father...but he wouldn't let me. It was like I had to choose sides. And as much as me and my father fought...I couldn't turn against him." He frowned. "Crazy, huh?"

"No. Understandable. You were in an impossible position." She pushed out a breath and was thoughtful for a moment. "When I met Maurice my world brightened even though I realized there was still a dark part in his soul. It didn't matter. He made me feel alive again. And as difficult as it was to break through all the walls he'd put up around himself, I still wanted to try because I knew deep down inside that the man underneath was worth it." She turned toward Rafe, searching his face in the dim light for understanding.

Rafe offered his rakish smile. "A Lawson trait with the ladies," he said, a tinge of humor in his voice.

"And now…I…I've ruined everything."

"Give him some time. He'll come around."

She slowly shook her head. "Not this time. You didn't see how he looked at me."

"No one could ever look at you and see anything but incredible, cher," he said.

Her gaze rose to meet his. "You'd say anything after a couple of glasses of bourbon."

He grinned. "You may be right."

She looked at him for a moment, seeing him in a brand-new light. "Thanks for the ride. And the talk. I'd better go."

Rafe opened his door and came around to open hers. He extended his hand and helped her out.

"Always the gentleman."

"Part of my Southern charm. And remember what I said."

She tilted her head to the side. "About what?"

"I'm always there for a lady in distress. Call if you need to," he said, his tone turning serious.

"Thank you. I will." She walked up the steps to her cottage.

The sun was beginning to crest over the horizon casting a soft orange glow across the gently rippling ocean as she turned and watched him drive away.

Layla closed the door behind her and the awful events of the evening came crashing down around her. She would do anything to change what had happened. She could only imagine what Maurice must be thinking, how betrayed he must feel. He'd trusted her.

Why didn't she tell him, prepare him, and let him make his own decision about attending the party? She tossed her purse on the bed. Her chest tightened. She knew why. It was for her own selfishness. It was her egotistical belief that she could fix things, heal things and that she could somehow do what no one else had been able to do. She hadn't been able to heal what was wrong between her and Brent, but she believed she could with Maurice and his family. And she screwed up.

Now he was gone and the rift between him and his family was wider than ever, and the gash she'd sliced through their relationship may never heal.

She sat down on the side of her bed then got right back up. She needed to talk to him. She'd make him listen.

Through the deep haze of a medicated induced sleep, the sounds of knocking seeped in. Maurice groaned, unable and unwilling to move for fear that the pain would return. Mercifully sleep gathered him back into its grip.

Layla knocked again. He had to be inside. His car was parked out front. She knocked louder. There were no lights on. She looked around. The last thing she needed was to cause a scene by waking the other guests. She knocked one last time.

Reluctantly she turned and walked away.

Layla awoke with a start. She shook her head to clear it then squinted at the nightstand clock. It was nearly ten. She sat up and untangled herself from the sheets. She was still fully clothed. She ran her hand over her face. When had she fallen asleep? Her thoughts were all foggy, but by degrees they all came into focus—the party, Maurice, the drive back with Rafe, going to Maurice's cottage. She squeezed her eyes shut then scrambled out of bed. The spa was scheduled to open in an hour but she had to talk to Maurice first.

Fresh from the shower, she dressed quickly, grabbed her tote bag and headed over to Maurice's. He was going to talk to her, he was going to listen even if she had to stand on his porch and scream how sorry she was.

When she crested the curve that led to his place the first thing that she noticed was that his car was not parked where it was the night before. Her heart jumped. She ran up the lane to the front door and knocked. She didn't hear a sound coming from inside. She ran around to the back of the house, hoping that he was there.

Her stomach knotted. The back deck was empty. She ran her hands through her hair then sprinted all the way to the main building. Breathless and with her heart pounding she approached the reception desk.

"Hello, Ms. Brooks," Gina greeted with a warm smile. "How can I help you?"

She swallowed. "Um, I was wondering if you could tell me if Mr. Lawson is still here." She forced a casual smile.

"Oh, you just missed him. He checked out about a half hour ago." She frowned. "Is everything all right?"

Layla blinked away the burn in her eyes. "Yes," she managed. "Fine. Thanks, Gina." She turned away slowly, fighting back the tears that threatened to spill with every breath that she took.

She opened the door to the spa an instant before the tears rolled down her cheeks. She locked the door behind her and wept.

* * *

"He still hasn't returned any of your calls?" Desiree asked as she walked with Layla along the beach.

Layla heaved a heavy sigh. "No. It's been almost a month. Not a word."

"Oh, sweetie." She put her arm around Layla's shoulders. "I wish I knew what I could do to make this right."

Layla hung her head. "So do I." She looked out across the water. "It would be so much easier if I didn't care, you know." Her voice cracked. "But I do, Desi, I care so damned much and I hurt him. I never meant to hurt him."

"I know, I know," she soothed, holding her close as they continued to walk.

"If I could just see him face-to-face, I know I could explain, try to get him to understand. That's all I want, the chance to let him know how sorry I am and that I never meant to hurt or deceive him. But I wouldn't even know where to begin to look. Brooklyn is a big place."

"The only advice I can offer is if and when he's ready he'll find you. And in the meantime you have us and a new life here and a new apartment that you need to get settled in."

"True," she breathed. "I have plenty to keep me busy."

"I'm really glad you decided to stay."

Layla turned to her friend. "Well, with you and

Mel twisting my arm, what choice did I have," she teased.

"That's what friends are for! As a matter of fact, one thing I do know for sure, a shopping spree always seems to help. Let's go into town and shop for your new place."

Her eyes crinkled with her smile. "Yes. Let's do that."

"I won't be coming back, Doc," Maurice said.

"I see." Dr. Morrison studied his tight expression. "I take it that you're all better. The pain, the anxiety, the nightmares…all gone."

His eyes flashed.

"Well?"

"I'll live with it."

"Is that the kind of life you want to live?"

"What choice do I have?" he barked, glaring at her.

"You do have a choice. There are always choices. You chose to give yourself a chance and you did when you went away. You found someone. We talked about her. Layla." He flinched at the sound of her name. "You finally came outside of yourself. You reconnected with Ross, too. Are you ready to cut him out again? You were happy, really happy, Maurice. I heard it in your voice, in everything that you said." She paused. "Why are you so ready to choose to let that go?"

The muscles in his face twitched. "She knew," he said quietly. "She knew how I felt and she used it against me."

"Your entire life has been built around not accepting mistakes or weakness in yourself or in others. It started with your father and continued throughout your life and especially your years in the Navy. As much as you disparage your father for his unbending views...you're doing the very same thing."

He started to protest.

"No. Listen. Layla made a mistake. A mistake that you have determined was intentional. She kicked down the barrier that you set up and you can't accept that. You can't accept a shred of weakness in someone that you love."

His eyes widened.

"Yes, love. You need to admit that to yourself. That's why it hurts so badly, Maurice because you love her. You loved your father and he hurt you by taking his own life and you can't forgive him. And until you can find that space inside yourself that is able to accept fault in others, accept weakness and mistakes—all the things that make us human—the pain will never leave. No one and nothing will be able to touch that space inside of you. The healing will never happen."

Chapter 24

Branford slowly hung up the phone. His position in politics over the years had afforded him a long arm, many friends, foes and favors. Today he'd reached out to his friend, the Secretary of the Navy. He should have done this long ago. He should have done it when he'd heard that his nephew had nearly died in Afghanistan. But he'd allowed his stubborn pride to get in the way.

Grudgingly he had to admit that his son was right. He'd lost his brother, David. He wouldn't lose his nephew, too. They were family first and foremost.

He stared out of his Capitol Hill office window. The iconic image of the White House faced him in the distance.

Maurice zipped his suitcase. The last bus for the day leaving for Sag Harbor left in a little more than an hour. It had taken days and nights of soul searching and days and nights of realizing that living the rest of his life without Layla in it was not what he wanted. He'd saved all of her phone messages. He'd listened to her asking him to call her, to let her explain.

Maybe if she would have him, he could make this right. He grabbed his keys and started out. He pulled open the door and stopped in his tracks.

"I knew if I called you wouldn't answer," Branford said. He glanced at the suitcase. "We need to talk. You deserve to know what happened to your father. I can have my driver take you wherever you want to go."

"How did you find me?" he asked, trying to recover from the shock of seeing his uncle at his front door.

"I have ways."

"I have a bus to catch," he said, but didn't make a move to leave.

"I can take you to the bus."

He never heard the tone in his uncle's voice before, contrite, pleading almost. And suddenly he was tired. Tired of fighting, tired of holding on to the anger.

He nodded in agreement. "All right." He stepped across the threshold and locked the door behind them.

The black Lincoln Town Car was parked in front

of his building. The driver came out and opened the door. Maurice got in first.

"Where to, sir?" the driver asked.

Branford turned to Maurice.

"Downtown Brooklyn. Court and Joralemon."

The car moved into traffic.

Maurice stared ahead. "You said you wanted to talk."

"You've blamed me for your father's death. And maybe you're right."

Maurice swung his head toward his uncle.

"But not in the way that you think..."

The twenty-minute ride wasn't enough time to mend the fragile fabric of their relationship. It was only a beginning. But finally hearing the truth from his uncle in all of its ugliness was the corner that he needed to turn. All these years he'd believed the note that he'd found in his father's bedroom. To this day he could still see the damning words...*I know how hard this will be for you, son, but there is no other way. I tried to make things right and the one person who I reached out to for help was my own brother and he turned his back on me. He turned his back on me when I needed him most. The one person who could have helped me...*

David had begged his brother to point the SEC away from him until he could figure out what to do, help him to find some way of covering his tracks. He knew that if he were caught and convicted he would spend the rest of his life in jail. He'd never survive that, he'd said. *You have to help me. You're my brother.* Those words tortured Branford's every waking hour. But what David was asking him to do went against every iota of integrity that he had. If he did what was being asked, he'd never be able to live with himself. He firmly believed in right and wrong and justice, and that real men stood up and dealt with their mistakes in life.

What was so bitterly ironic was that it was Branford's sense of pride, integrity and morality that catapulted him to the heights of his political career were the same attributes that destroyed two brothers. And the same attributes that ultimately repaired the untold damage that David Lawson had wielded when he'd swindled billions of dollars from his clients.

No one knew. There had been rumors of course. But they were stamped out as quickly as they arose. It was Branford who made sure of that, using his connections and his power to ensure that what his brother had done would never become public knowledge to tarnish his memory. And it was Branford's fortune that had repaid David's victims over the past decade. In silence.

"Why didn't you ever say anything?"

Branford shook his head. "I made a promise that what happened would not get out. Those who were hurt by him swore never to reveal what happened as long as restitution was made. And it has been." He lifted his chin and stared ahead. "But at a cost that money will never repay." He turned to his nephew and reached over to tentatively cover his nephew's hand with his own. "We lost you in the process. You're my brother's son. You have a family, Maurice. And whenever you're ready we're here for you."

Maurice's nostrils flared as he tried to breathe over the tightness in his throat. "Thank you," he managed.

The car came to a stop.

The two men held each other with a look.

"You're going to miss your bus," Branford said gruffly.

And if Maurice wasn't mistaken, his uncle looked a bit misty-eyed. He grabbed his bag from between his feet and got out of the car.

He walked slowly toward the bus and the dull, deep soul pain that had been a constant companion began to ease. If he could make things right with Layla perhaps it would be gone for good.

Branford watched him board the bus and the weight that he'd been carrying for so many years lifted. Maybe now it was time to tell his sister, Jacqueline, the truth as well.

Chapter 25

Layla locked up behind her last client for the day and began cleaning up. She'd fallen into a livable routine in the months that she'd been living in Sag Harbor. Her days were filled with work and her evenings with walks on the beach, dinner with friends or curled up with a good book.

She was almost settled in her new place, and with a few more purchases she was sure she'd have it just the way she wanted. Yet, there wasn't a day that went by that she didn't think of Maurice and what they almost had. She stopped trying to call and had resigned herself to the idea that it was over. At some point she would be able to truly move on. But for now it was one day at a time.

She went to turn off the lights when the knock on her door stopped her. She rolled her eyes in annoyance and walked over with the intention of being as nice but as firm as possible about hours and appointments. She pulled up the shade that covered the glass window of the door and her heart stood still.

Her hands shook as she fumbled to unlock the door. She pulled it open and stood there unable to move, afraid to breathe. Her heart pounded.

"I should have called and made an appointment." He hesitantly reached out and tucked her hair behind her ear.

She blinked rapidly to keep the tears at bay.

"I should have listened. I should have stayed."

"I never meant to hurt you," she said, her voice cracking with emotion.

"I know that now. I know a lot of things now. You touched me in all the places that needed healing. And most of all I know how much I love you, Layla. I love you and I can't spend another day without you."

Her heart exploded with joy as she flung herself into his arms.

Maurice wrapped her in his embrace, his mouth finding hers, finding his way home and vowing never to lose his way again.

He nuzzled her neck, inhaled her scent, whispered over and again his love for her and absorbed her words of love in return. "There's so much I have to tell you," he whispered.

She cupped his face in her hands and gazed up into his adoring eyes. "We have all the time in the world." She took his hand, shut the door and led him to the back room where the healing all began.

Chapter 26

"One of these days the guests are going to figure out what *really* goes on in here," Maurice murmured against Layla's neck as they stepped out of the shower together.

"Then I'll just have to charge more," she said over her giggles and tucked the towel securely around her body.

Maurice put his arm around her waist as they walked back to the massage room where they'd left their clothing.

"A lot has changed…since…you left," she began tentatively. She glanced up to gauge his reaction. She lifted her panties from the chair and wiggled into them before dropping her towel.

Maurice swallowed, his eyes eating her up from head to toe. "Not that I can tell," he said in a rough voice.

She made a face. "This," she waved her hand along the length of her body, "is not what I'm talking about."

"Oh. My bad." He grinned mischievously. He shrugged into a white cotton shirt and zipped his jeans. "You gonna tell me or do you want me to guess?"

Layla fastened the snap on her shorts. "I bought a little place out here."

His fingers stopped buttoning his shirt. His right brow rose in question. "So…you're planning to stay out here."

She nodded. "There was nothing for me back in the city and when you left…I…" Her voice trailed off.

Maurice stepped up to her. He lifted her chin with the tip of his finger. "I think I've finally reached a place in my life where moving forward is the plan for the day. That means accepting that there is only so much I can do about what has happened in the past, and I have to make the most of the present *and* the future." He paused a moment. "I want to include you in my present and my future…if that's what you want."

She blinked away the sudden burn of impending tears in her eyes. "I want to," she managed.

He reached out and tucked behind her ear the forever-wayward strand of hair from her face. Slowly, he leaned down and kissed her tenderly on the lips. "Brooklyn is only a car ride away," he said softly.

Her heart pounded like crazy in her chest. Her smile wavered at the corners. "True."

"But, I'm here now."

"For how long?"

"A couple of days. I need to get back."

She nodded. "Bills to pay," she said tongue in cheek.

"Yeah, unfortunately, my father's will, after what he'd done, was pretty much only a lot of words on paper." He shook his head and sighed heavily. "He'd made some really bad investments, lost everything and then began using his clients' money to pay back clients. It was a real shell game. I knew he was having some trouble...but I never imagined..."

Layla gently touched his upper arm. "I'm sorry."

"So am I," he said on a heavy breath of regret. "And I'm sorry that it took me so long to want to hear the truth." He took her hand and they started out.

"What made you change your mind?" she asked as they stepped out of the spa and into the corridor that wound around the main complex of the resort.

"Let's talk about it out of here."

She grinned up at him. "I like the sound of that."

He reached around her and pulled open the glass-and-chrome door to the lounge area of the main building.

Several guests were milling around in the common areas and a young couple that had "newlywed" written all over them was checking in at the reception desk.

"Are you staying here?" Layla asked, realizing that it was Labor Day weekend and she was pretty sure The Port was at capacity.

"Naw. I wasn't able to get a room. I'm staying in town."

She stopped and turned to him. "I have plenty of space on one side of a very comfy queen-sized bed."

His eyes darkened. "I have to warn you, I sleep in the nude."

Her smile widened. "I remember." She tugged on her bottom lip with her teeth for a moment. "I have one condition."

"Condition?"

"Yes. When I wake up in the morning, I want you to be there," she said softly.

"For as long as you'll have me, you'll never have to worry about that again."

"Promise me," she said, almost breathless.

Maurice cupped her face in his palms and looked deep into her eyes. "I promise."

Layla's eyes moved slowly over his face, taking in every edible detail. *Lawd, how she'd missed this man*. She hadn't believe she'd ever feel this way about anyone again. But she did, and when she thought she'd lost him for good... Well, he was back now and that was what was important. *Live in the present and for the future*. That would be their motto from now on.

"Let's go into town and get your things."

"My one bag is with the concierge. They're holding it for me."

"Here?"

"Yep. I didn't stop at the hotel on my way in. I'd taken long enough. All these weeks…I didn't want to waste another minute not finding you, seeing you again."

Layla pressed her lips together to keep them from trembling. She swallowed over the tightness in her throat. "Then I guess we'd better get your bag."

They strolled along the pathway and away from The Port, turned onto another winding road that led to her new home.

"There's been something I've been meaning to ask you for a long time. And if we're going to make a go of this, I don't want anything hanging out there to linger between us." She took a quick glance at him.

"Ask me anything."

"One day I saw you with Kim…Fleming. It looked like you were arguing." She hesitated. "What was going on?"

He heaved a deep breath. "That's complicated."

"Too complicated to tell me?"

"No." He waited a beat. "I knew her husband. We were on the failed mission together."

Her stomach clenched and she grabbed his hand and gently squeezed it.

"She said she recognized me from a photo that her husband had sent to her. She wanted to know what happened that night. She said the Navy wouldn't tell her anything. She wanted to know if I was with him, if we were together. She wanted to know everything." He glanced away. "All of our missions are covert. I was bound by an oath that I took. I wanted to tell her," his voice cracked, "but I couldn't. I still can't." He lowered his head and pushed out a breath. "Just like I can't tell you why we were there, only that we were. And if you didn't see us together, I wouldn't have told you that I even knew her husband. There isn't a day that goes by that I wished things were different."

Layla stopped walking and turned to him. "I know how difficult it is for you. But I can't tell you how much I admire the man that you are. Even though telling her the truth would have eased your conscience you didn't do it because of your own moral center. I couldn't ask for more than that from a man."

He gave her a short smile. "Thank you."

"No. Thank you."

Layla opened the door to her quaint one-bedroom house that overlooked the rocky shore.

Maurice stepped inside and closed the door behind them. "Very nice," he said, looking around at the inviting space.

Sheer floor-to-ceiling curtains in off-white blew gently in the partially opened window. The open layout gave an immediate view of the living and dining space and modern stainless-steel kitchen. The low smoked glass tables, and the taupe-colored microfiber sectional and ottoman sat on gleaming hardwood floors. Accents of candy apple red, gold and sea foam green played out in soft throws, pillows, pottery and vases filled with flowers.

"Thanks," she said, turning toward him with a bright smile. "You can put your things in my room." She angled her head toward the bedroom and he followed her around the short corner.

Layla opened the door and there was an instant feeling of calm that permeated throughout the room and embraced them. Everything about it was soothing, from the soft palette to the spare furnishings. Every surface was clear except for vases filled with blooming flora in vibrant bursts of tropical colors. The aromatic air only added to the sense of serenity.

She slid open the door to her closet. "You can unpack if you want. I can make space in one of my drawers and you can hang what you want in here."

Maurice placed his overnight bag at his feet. "This is a great place, Layla. It's you."

She tipped her head to the side. "Me?"

"Yes." He crossed the room and stepped up to her.

"Soft and inviting." He leaned down and kissed her lightly on the lips.

Her heart fluttered. She drew in a breath. "I still have a few things I want to do, but it's coming along. I'm getting used to things…a new life."

He looked into her eyes. "Me too."

Her warm brown eyes moved slowly over his face, recommitting every plane to memory. "I can tell."

"Can you?"

"Yes." She stepped away and turned toward the chaise longue that was in front of the window. She sat down. "Your aura is different. The tension that hovered around you like a storm cloud is almost gone. There is a light in your eyes now, an easier tone in your voice." She paused a moment, gauging her words. "Your leg…the limp is barely noticeable."

His mouth moved into a half smile. "Very observant, Ms. Brooks," he teased.

"How's the pain?"

His chest rose and fell. "I haven't taken any pain medication in weeks. I've been sleeping better. The nightmares…one in the past month." He studied her expression that remained fixed on him—open and waiting. "I finally started listening to what Dr. Morrison and you have been telling me all along." He sat down next to her on the chaise. He linked his fingers together and lowered his head while he collected his thoughts.

"My uncle came to see me just before I was leaving to come here."

Layla's body tensed.

Maurice angled his head toward her. "We talked, finally. We really talked." He told her what Branford had revealed and how his heartfelt confession was another part of the broken pieces of his life that were coming back together. "I'd been holding on to so much anger and rage and irrational feelings of betrayal." He looked directly at her and her breathing tightcned. "It's like you and Dr. Morrison have been saying all along, I'll never get past it and heal until I can let it go."

"Have you?" she asked softly.

He nodded his head. "Something Dr. Morrison said brought it all home."

"What was that?"

"She said that the root of it all was that I loved my father, and I believed that what he did was a betrayal of that love." He turned fully toward her and took her hand in his. "And that I love you and that's why I flipped when I thought you'd betrayed me."

Her pulsed pounded. *Love*. Did he say love?

"I love you, Layla, more than I ever realized. I love you and I want to use every day ahead of us to remind you how much."

"Are you sure?" she asked, her voice wobbly.

"I've never been more certain of anything in my life."

She leaned forward and draped her arms around his neck. "I think I fell in love with you the moment I touched you," she whispered.

Maurice threaded his fingers through her hair, cupped the back of her head and eased her toward him. "It won't be easy," he said.

"Nothing in life is."

"You were meant for me," he said in a strained almost faraway voice. "This is going to sound crazy, but…when my plane went down and we were trapped in those mountains…there were moments when I didn't think I would make it." He swallowed. "But I kept seeing this light." He squinted as if trying to bring the vision into focus. "It gave me hope that everything would be okay. And then I came here and the first time that I saw you, from a distance walking along the path, I saw that light again, radiating all around you." He slowly shook his head. "I thought I was seeing things. But I wasn't. I was seeing hope and it was *you*."

Tears of joy filled her eyes and slid over her lids onto her cheeks.

Maurice leaned closer and kissed away her tears.

Layla pulled him to her. Her soul sang with unbridled happiness.

Their kiss was new, sweet, bursting with hope and possibility. And when they christened her bed with their pledge of love and fidelity, they understood that today was the beginning of the rest of their lives.

Epilogue

As the summer wound down, Maurice spent his weeks in New York and his weekends at Layla's. She'd made several trips into the city and met his friend Ross and Ross's wife, Janet, whom she loved on sight. So, of course they were in attendance at Melanie's end-of-season party.

"You really lucked out, my man," Ross was saying as he stood next to Maurice on the deck.

Maurice looked out to where Layla was laughing with Melanie, Desiree and Janet. He grinned. "Yeah, I am lucky." He draped his arm around Ross's shoulder. "I wanted to run something by you."

"Shoot." He took a swallow of his drink.

"Layla and I have been talking about opening

a therapeutic center for injured vets out here. Desiree and Lincoln are all for it. I've been taking some
counseling classes and I know that I can connect
with vets who have been injured and are trying to
readjust, and Layla has the physical therapy skills…"

"Wow. Heavy undertaking. But I know you two
can do it. Any way that I can help?"

Maurice grinned. "I'm sure I'll think of something."

"What are you two conspiring about?" Layla
asked with a smile as she walked up to them.

Maurice slid his arm around her waist and pulled
her close.

"Planning on healing the world, one man at a
time," he said before leaning down to kiss her.

She gazed up into the eyes of the man she adored
beyond reason and knew that the healing of *her* man
had already begun.

* * * * *

We hope you enjoyed reading
TOUCH ME NOW by Donna Hill,
the third book in SAG HARBOR VILLAGE *series.*
In Donna Hill's upcoming
Harlequin Kimani Romance,
EVERYTHING IS YOU,
we'll revisit the popular Lawson family,
and we've included the first three chapters
for your review.

Chapter 1

A yellow cab turned onto South Figueroa and eased to a stop in front of the Beacon Hill Towers. Jacqueline Lawson stepped out into the late, balmy Los Angeles afternoon. The red-vested doorman pulled open the glass-and-chrome door of the condominium as she approached.

"Afternoon, Ms. Lawson."

Jacqueline smiled but it didn't reach her eyes that were hidden behind wide, dark shades. Her maple brown skin glistened in the June sun. "Hi, Bobby. Hot out here today."

"Yes, ma'am. They say thunderstorms."

"How's your wife and daughter?" she asked, stepping into the cool embrace of the lobby.

"They're well. Thanks. There's a package for you at the front desk."

"Thanks, Bobby." She adjusted her tote bag over her shoulder. Her teal colored sling back heels tapped out a slow by steady rhythm against the terra-cotta floor. She approached the concierge desk. "Hi, Mike. Bobby said I have a package."

"Sure do. Would you like me to send it up? It's kind of heavy."

"Yes, please. Send it up later. Thanks." She started off toward the elevator and the room swayed. She slowed her step and drew in a steadying breath. The warning words of her doctor echoed in her head. Concentrating, she walked to the bank of elevators. Exhaustion rode through her in waves. She squeezed her eyes closed for a moment and willed herself to remain upright.

The elevator dinged and the polished stainless-steel doors silently slid open. A young, very tanned couple exited, gave brief nods and moved past her.

Jacqueline stepped inside, thankful to be alone as the doors closed behind her. She leaned against the back wall for support. She was running out of time and her options were limited.

The doors slid open on the eighteenth floor and Jacqueline pushed herself forward down the hallway that was decorated with fresh flowers on antique tabletops and black-and-white art on the walls. Her two-bedroom apartment was at the end of the hall that she shared with one other tenant.

Once inside, she adjusted the cooling system and walked into her bedroom that opened onto a panoramic view of downtown Los Angeles.

Item by item she stripped out of her clothes and tossed them into a hamper in the bathroom. She took her silk robe from a hook on the back of the door and slid it on, tying the belt loosely around her waist.

She needed to lie down. The simple trip to the doctor's office had drained her more than she'd anticipated. She stretched out on the bed and then turned onto her side curling into a half-fetal position.

That's the way Raymond found her when he came in an hour later, carrying the box that had been delivered earlier.

He placed the box in the corner near the chaise longue and quietly approached. He leaned down and placed a feathery light kiss on her forehead. She stirred ever so slightly, murmuring something that he could not make out. He eased out of the room and shut the bedroom door halfway, deciding to surprise her with an early dinner. He took a quick shower, changed into his favorite weather-worn navy blue sweatpants and padded barefoot into the living space that opened onto the kitchen. He crossed the gleaming hardwood floor to the entertainment unit. The gleam of Jacqueline's Associated Press Medal for photojournalism sat in its place of honor encased in glass. Every time he looked at it a feeling of pride puffed his chest, reminding him of what an incredible woman she was and the fearlessness that it took for her to earn it. He turned on the stereo to his favorite R & B station.

Since their return from their last assignment in the rain forests of the Amazon, Jacqueline had been quiet and withdrawn. Initially, he thought she was worn-out from the grueling three months of the trip or that she'd caught a bug. But she insisted that she was fine.

Raymond pulled open the double door stainless-steel refrigerator and opened the vegetable bin drawer. He took out fresh spinach, baby tomatoes, a box of mushrooms and a cucumber and prepared a quick side salad. Jacqueline loved pasta and it was the one thing he was good at in the kitchen. He washed and deveined a half pound of shrimp and then sautéed fresh garlic in a light olive oil. He tossed the cleaned shrimp into the sizzling pan, while the water boiled for the pasta.

"Hey."

Raymond turned from the sink. He smiled at her still sleepy-eyed appearance. "Hey, yourself. Get enough rest?"

She nodded her head, covered her yawn and tightened the belt on her robe. "What are you doing?"

"Fixing dinner. Figured you'd be hungry. I know I am." He plucked a shrimp from the pan and walked over to her. He held it tauntingly above her lips. She opened her mouth and he dropped it in.

She chewed slowly. "Hmmm."

He grinned. "It'll be ready soon."

She sat down on the counter stool. "How long have you been here?"

"Hmm about an hour or so." He dropped the pasta into the boiling water and then opened the refrigerator and took out a bottle of beer. "Want one?" he asked, holding up a bottle of Rochefort Trappistes 10.

Jacqueline propped her chin up on her hands. "A new one?"

"Yeah, and you'll love it. It's a Belgium brew." His smooth brows bounced.

Besides being an award-winning photographer, Raymond was a beer connoisseur and collector. His house in the valley had a room with some of the most rare and expensive beers in the world. He'd been featured in *All About Beer* and *Beer Connoisseur* magazines on several occasions. And whatever part of the world that they traveled he always had to try out the beer.

He opened a bottle and handed it to her. He watched her in anticipation while she took her first sip. Her eyes fluttered closed as she savored the dark color, full-bodied taste with hints of strong plum, raisin, and black currant.

"Hmmm," she hummed in appreciation, rolling the liquid around on her tongue. She'd always been a white wine and martini girl, but Raymond had expanded her taste buds. In her head beer was baseball, hot dogs and a six-pack. He turned beer drinking into an exotic experience.

Raymond clapped his hands. "Great. I knew you'd love it." He turned back to the stove, took the pasta off the flame and drained it in the sink. He mixed chopped baby tomatoes, fresh basil, olive oil and ground black pepper, and tossed it with the pasta in a large serving plate. He took the cooked shrimp from the skillet, layered them on top then sprinkled the dish with fresh parmesan cheese.

Jacqueline got up and took two plates down from the cabinet over the sink. Raymond seized the opportunity of her close proximity to slide his arm around her waist and plant a kiss behind her ear. She moved easily away.

"I'm actually starved," she said, not looking at him while she put the plates on the counter.

Raymond watched the way she kept her back to him, the calculated way that she placed each item next to the other.

"So…what did you do today?" he asked, giving the pasta one last toss.

For a moment she stilled. "Met Traci for brunch," she said a bit too cheerfully. "She asked about you." She looked at him quickly before turning away.

Raymond brought the plate to the counter along with the serving tongs. "Salad is in the fridge."

"I'll get it."

They sat down opposite each other and dished out the pasta.

"Looks and smells delicious," Jacqueline said, staying focused on her plate.

Raymond studied her from beneath his lashes. "When are you going to tell me what's going on with you?"

"What do you mean?"

"You know what I mean, Jacquie. You're tired all the time, you barely want me to touch you, you won't hold a real conversation... Do I need to go on? You haven't been the same since we got back."

She blinked rapidly, reached for her bottle of beer but put it down. "Ray..." She pushed out a breath.

"Say it. Say what you've been trying *not* to say for weeks."

She looked at him, stared deep into his eyes and saw her own hurt and confusion swimming in the dark depths.

"I'm tired. Plain and simple. Can't I be tired? I'm not superwoman, you know. I've been working non-stop for the past year in every nook and cranny on the planet," she said, throwing her hand up in the air. "And the last thing I need is you bugging me to death about it." She took a long swallow of beer and set it down then ran her hand through the spiral twists of her hair. She turned her head away. "I'm sorry." She looked at him. "Can we enjoy this nice meal that you toiled over and talk about something else?" She offered a strained smile. "Please."

Raymond exhaled a long frustrated breath. "You're a difficult woman, J," he conceded. "But I'll let it go."

"Good." She turned her attention to her pasta. "You want me to drive you to the airport in the morning?"

"Would you?"

"Of course."

"I wish you would change your mind and come with me. It's my folks fiftieth anniversary, J. How often does that happen?"

She kept her eyes on her plate. "I told you, I don't do family."

"You never talk about your family."

"Nothing to talk about." She stirred her food around on her plate.

"Another non-topic," he murmured.

Jacqueline chose to ignore the barb. She'd put physical miles and emotional distance between her and her family for years. She periodically stayed in touch with her nieces, LeAnn, Dominique and Desiree, and nephews Rafe and Justin. But she hadn't spoken to her brother in years. She was not of the mighty Lawson ilk. She made her own name and her own way in the world. She refused to be dictated to by her brother the way he did everyone else. The people in her life didn't even know that she was related to the royal Lawson clan of Louisiana. And that's the way she wanted to keep it, including Raymond.

Raymond studied her while he finished off his beer. What happened between her and her brother? She never talked about Branford Lawson and had he not done some digging on his own he would have never known that they were related. Crazy. But he would respect her wishes, even if he didn't understand her reasons. To him, family was sacred. He came from a large, loving, all-in-your-business family. He couldn't imagine not having them in his life. But Jacqueline Lawson was a complex woman. It was what he loved about her, but he'd kept that to himself as well.

Jacqueline pushed up from the table and came around to Raymond's side. She put her arm around his waist and rested her head on his shoulder. "You're going to have a wonderful time, do all those things that families do when they get together and then you'll fly back."

Raymond turned on the stool and pulled her between his thighs. He looked up at her and caressed the side of her face with his finger. She lowered herself onto his lap. He tilted her chin upward and kissed her softly.

Jacqueline lightly draped her wrists on either side of his neck and looked into his eyes, seeing the history of their journey there, a journey that she was going to have to end. Her insides tightened.

When had their relationship gone from professional to personal? For several years it had been only business between them. It was the way it should have stayed, but she'd made the mistake of letting Raymond slip past her defenses.

They'd met quite by accident at the National Association of Black Journalists in '09, at the annual awards dinner in Washington, D.C....

Chapter 2

Jacqueline never enjoyed those stuffed shirt affairs. She'd sweltered in them most of her young life growing up in the Lawson household where the sun shining was reason enough to throw a gala. Her mother and father—God rest their souls—were Southern royalty. Her father's closest friends were those that most people only read about. And her mother was in her glory entertaining them. The Lawson home was and remained the central hub for the comings and goings of the political, corporate and entertainment Who's Who. And her brothers Branford and David were cut from the same cloth.

Perhaps it was because she was the youngest—a change-of-life baby, as her mother always reminded her—and a girl that her father focused all of his attention on her brothers, and her mother turned her over to the nanny so that she could conduct her charity events and social climbing.

Jacqueline never felt part of the family but more of an afterthought. So, she made her own way, built her own life and over time the tenuous ties that bound her to her family were severed. The final cut being her brother David.

Unfortunately, these once per year events were part and parcel of her business and as reluctant as she was to admit it, she did learn from living it, that rubbing elbows was needed and necessary. And, besides, it was one of the few times that she did have a chance to interact with her colleagues and see some of the important work they were doing and being recognized for.

When she walked into the grand ballroom at the Kennedy Center, she immediately wished that she'd brought a date. She pasted on her best smile and wandered over to the bar. The crutch of a glass of white wine could hold her up for at least an hour if she sipped really slowly. And if she found a comfortable leaning position or a good seat out of the way, her feet encased in "sex me" heels would last through the long evening.

"You look like you hate this almost as much as I do."

She angled her head to the right and inhaled a

short, sharp breath. *Yummy,* was her first thought before she could respond.

"Is it that obvious?" She arched a questioning brow as her photographic eye took him in from head to toe in one click of her internal lens.

The amazing honey brown eyes twinkled in the light and creased at the edges when he smiled down at her. She wasn't a big gospel fan but he sure could be a body double for the singer BeBe Winans with the dulcet tone to go with the look. And that body appeared totally comfortable and sleek in his tux.

"You have the ever-ready wineglass. The casual lean against the bar pose…" His gaze traveled down. "…to keep the pressure off of those pretty feet."

She bit back a smile.

"And the…'just how long is this thing gonna last?' look in your eyes." He turned to the bar and picked up his glass of Hennessy on the rocks then returned his attention back to her.

"Observant."

"Occupational hazard. Journalist?"

"Photographic."

He nodded slowly in appreciation.

"You?"

"Foreign correspondent."

She switched her wine flute from her right hand to her left and extended her hand. "Jacqueline."

"Raymond Jordan." His hand enveloped hers. He smelled good, too. "Nice to meet you."

"You have a table?"

"No. Do you?"

"Naw." He took a swallow of his drink. "I figured there had to be an available seat in here somewhere. After all, I pay my dues and I did get an invite."

She giggled. "My sentiments exactly."

"Care to spend the evening with another jaded guest?"

Jacqueline glanced up at him. "Sure, why not."

Raymond crooked his elbow and Jacqueline hooked her arm through.

They found a table in the center of the room with two empty seats at a table for eight. After a bit of seat shifting they settled next to each other and were soon served appetizers for the sit-down dinner.

Up front, CNN Correspondent Anderson Cooper was in conversation with Karen Ballard who specialized in motion picture photography. Jacqueline and Raymond whispered conspiratorially about Cooper's appearance in a film, and they entertained themselves by concocting stories about the plethora of attendees that spanned the gamut of journalism, and swapped stories about some of their memorable assignments.

Raymond was equally as traveled as Jacqueline and spoke three languages fluently, compared to her two. He'd lived in Japan for a year, spent several summers in Europe and loved motorcycle riding.

"What was it like being embedded with the troops in Iraq?" he asked.

"Scary. But I knew that they wouldn't let anything happen to me. I was there to do a job and they respected that." She glanced off.

"Must have been tough. The things you saw..."

She nodded. "It was." She turned and looked into his eyes. "The sad part is, I've seen and photographed worse."

"I know. In this business when you think you've seen everything, there's one more thing that sucks the air out of your lungs."

"Fortunately, there's still some beauty left in the world."

"Fortunately," he said and raised his glass to her, his gaze moving with appreciation across her face.

After a long line of award-winners and acceptance speeches, the event wound down to a glittering close.

Jacqueline and Raymond made their way out through the throng of bodies.

"Going to the after party?" Raymond asked once they stepped outside.

"Oh no," she said, waving her hand. "I've had enough party people to last me at least until this time next year."

Raymond chuckled. "Live here or staying in town?"

"Actually, I'm only here until tomorrow. I fly out in the morning. Off to Israel for the next month."

"Busy lady. Where do you call home?"

She hesitated for a moment. Louisiana was where she was born, but it hadn't been home for a very long time. "California."

His head jerked back in surprise. "Me, too."

"That's just a pickup line, right?"

"No." He chuckled. "Seriously. I moved out there about a year ago from Maplewood, New Jersey. I'm in San Fernando Valley. Been there about two years now."

"Hmmm. Small world."

"Maybe we can get together the next time we're in the same time zone."

Jacqueline offered a half smile. She lifted her arm to signal for the next taxi in line.

A cab pulled up in front of them. Raymond stepped forward and opened the door for her. She ducked into the cab.

Raymond stuck his head in. "Safe travels, pretty lady. Thanks for spending the evening with me."

There was no room in her life for a man like Raymond, for any man or anyone. She didn't stay put long enough for a relationship to have any meaning. And there was no point in opening the door to something that would never get a chance to cross the threshold.

"Take care," she said and for a brief instant, she wished things could be different, but they weren't.

Raymond gave her a wistful parting smile, shut the door and stepped back.

She watched him in the rearview mirror until the cab turned the corner. She was sure that was the last time she would see him, and in the ensuing months she often wondered what part of the world he was in. Sometimes she would run across his byline only to realize that he was a half a world away.

And then one day, there he was in the Khan el-Khalili market in Cairo, thousands of miles away from where they'd met nearly a year earlier.

"Ray?" She approached from his right. He turned and swiped his dark shades from his eyes. His grin spread like the sun rising over the ocean and moved through her.

"Jacquie, what in the world…"

She giggled like a schoolgirl. "You stole my line."

He tossed his head back and laughed from deep in his belly. "This is one of those crazy surprises…a good one," he added. He put down the bolt of white cotton that he'd been considering purchasing. "You look…different."

"Must be the sneakers," she teased.

He snapped his fingers. "That's it!" He stepped closer. "How long are you here for?"

"At least another two weeks. You?"

"Me too. I'm on assignment to cover the Summit."

"So am I," she said, inexplicably happy.

"Have any free time on your schedule? Maybe we can have dinner or do the tourist thing."

"Yeah," she nodded. "I'd like that."

"Where are you staying?"

"The Semiramis Intercontinental."

"I'm at the Atlas Zamalez. Are you free later tonight?"

"I have to caption some photos, but that should only take a few hours. How about eight?"

"No problem. I'll come by your hotel."

She bobbed her head. "Okay. I'll meet you in the lobby." She took a step back. "I, uh, have some errands to run so…I'll see you at eight."

"Eight."

She turned to leave.

"Hey, Jacquie."

She looked back over her shoulder. "You never told me your last name."

"Lawson."

Chapter 3

"Hey," Raymond said softly, moving his head back and forth in front of her.

Jacqueline blinked away the past and Ray came back into focus. She forced a smile.

"Where did you just go?"

She blew out a breath and shook her shoulders a bit. "I just realized that I didn't get to open my package." She took his hand and pulled him to his feet. "Come, I want to show you."

"Is it more equipment, J?" How many times had he watched her face light up when she discovered a new use for a lens or composed a picture a different way or purchased the latest waterproof camera? And how many times had he wished that he'd seen the same kind of excitement in her eyes for him? It came only in flashes, nothing ever sustained. And when it did, she would shut it down, turn off the lights as if she was afraid he would see whatever it was that she was trying to hide.

"Hush, and just come on."

They trooped into her bedroom and she went over to the box that Raymond had placed in the corner.

She duck-walked it over to the side table near the bed. "It *isn't* heavy, just awkward." Her long slender fingers quickly stripped the box of the securing tape and pulled open the flaps.

Reverently she reached inside and took out the first box that contained the jaw dropping Canon EOS 5D Mark III. Gingerly she removed it from its packaging and placed it on the table. The second box contained the equally spectacular new Nikon D800. Even Raymond had to admit he was impressed. These were top-of-the-line cameras and together cost more than six thousand dollars.

The remaining contents were a camera bag, lenses, and memory cards. Where many women splurged on clothes and shoes, Jacqueline poured her extra cash on photographic equipment. She said it was an investment in her business. And she was right. Her equipment alone was worth millions and she had the perfect piece ready for any assignment. Not only did she purchase the latest in photographic equipment, she was a collector of antique cameras as well. She had one room of her two-bedroom condo dedicated to her equipment.

"Impressive," Raymond murmured in appreciation. He picked up the Nikon and held it up to his face, adjusting the lens to take in the room. The powerful lens brought the skyline of Los Angeles into sharp relief.

"Nice," he said, drawing out the word. "Very nice." He gently put the camera down and turned to Jacqueline who was examining the Canon.

She glanced up at him. There was that smile, but he knew it wasn't for him but for her toys.

"At some point you are going to run out of space," he teased.

"Yeah, I've been thinking the same thing." She shrugged off the prospect. Running out of space would mean either giving up some of her toys or moving. She didn't relish either idea. She'd been approached on several occasions to donate some of her antique cameras to museums. That was always an option.

A shadow slowly crept over the room as if the lights were dimmed, followed by a bright flash of light just above the skyline. Jacqueline gasped at the boom that sounded like the bombs they'd both heard and lived through in war-torn countries.

She momentarily shut her eyes against the frightening noise. Raymond hurried over to the French doors that were blown open onto the terrace. He

fought against the wind and lashing rain that fero-
ciously beat down everything in its path to get the
doors closed.

He managed to pull the doors shut but not without a cost. He turned slowly around.

Jacqueline hid her giggle behind her hand. Just
that quickly he was drenched from head to foot.

"Let me get you a towel." She scampered off to the
linen closet and brought back a towel to find Raymond pulling his T-shirt over his head and stepping
out of his damp sweatpants.

There was nothing to say about Ray's physique
other than perfection. He was toned from his work-
outs but also from the hard and fast life that he lived.
Traversing mountains, slicing his way through tropical jungles, treading across rushing rivers were all
as common to him as another man who went to the
office in a suit and tie.

She wished that she could say that was the only
attraction, that it was only physical. It wasn't. That's
what made this all so painfully hard. Would she ever
stop wanting him, needing him? Her chest tightened
while a flash of how empty her life would be without Raymond in it ran through her.

She walked up to him and tenderly stroked his
face with the towel, then across his broad shoulders
and down his bare chest.

Raymond clasped her by the wrists and pulled her
flush against him.

"When am I ever going to stop wanting you," he growled deep in his throat. He cupped her face in his hands and swept down to kiss her. A hungry longing roared through him the way it always did when he touched her.

Jacqueline moaned against his mouth. Her body instantly responded to the fire that he lit in her belly. She moved closer, parted her lips to let him in. She wrapped her arms around him, giving into her need this one last time. Her heart thundered as the rain pounded against the windows.

Raymond lifted her off her feet and walked with her to her bed.

It was all so familiar yet different every time that he touched her, made her body come alive in new ways. Her skin sang beneath his fingertips and her insides vibrated with desire. His mouth was hot and wet and everywhere that it touched it set her ablaze.

When he entered her, the world came apart in a million little pieces. And with each thrust, every kiss, touch and moan the pieces came together and exploded again and again.

The sky lit up beyond them and her body swirled around him like the wicked wind and his love poured into her like the falling rain.

Jacqueline fought back her tears and held him to her, listening to the familiar beat of his heart, knowing that this was the last time.

* * * * *

Have yourself a sexy little holiday
with three favorite authors in...

Merry SEXY CHRISTMAS

BEVERLY JENKINS
KAYLA PERRIN
MAUREEN SMITH

May your days—and nights—be merry and bright
with these brand-new stories, written by three of the
genre's hottest authors, perfect for adding a dash of
sizzle to the Christmas season!

Available November 2012 wherever books are sold!

REQUEST YOUR FREE BOOKS!

2 FREE NOVELS
PLUS 2 FREE GIFTS!

KIMANI™
ROMANCE

Love's ultimate destination!

Only one man can satisfy her craving…

KIMANI ROMANCE

PHYLLIS BOURNE

Taste for Temptation

Taste for TEMPTATION

PHYLLIS BOURNE

After being left at the altar, Brandi Collins plans to undergo a major transformation. But how is she supposed to shed pounds with the tempting smell of chocolate wafting into her condo? It's handsome hunk and pastry chef Adam Ellison who's creating the irresistible confections. Now only one thing will satisfy Adam's craving for Brandi….

KIMANI **HOTTIES**
It's All About Our Men

Available November 2012 wherever books are sold!